DEATH BY SOUP

For my wife Suzanne,
you're SOOOO soup-er!

Kelpies is an imprint of Floris Books
First published in 2018 by Floris Books
Text © 2018 David MacPhail. Illustrations © 2018 Floris Books

David MacPhail and Laura Aviñó have asserted their rights
under the Copyright, Designs and Patent Act 1988 to be
identified as the Author and Illustrator of this Work

The publisher acknowledges subsidy from
Creative Scotland towards the publication of this volume

 Also available as an eBook

British Library CIP data available
ISBN 978-178250-516-7
Printed in Poland

DEATH BY SOUP

DAVID MACPHAIL
ILLUSTRATED BY LAURA AVIÑÓ

Kelpies

The Soggy Beginning

It was raining in Glasgow, which shouldn't come as a surprise. It's a bit like saying it's sunny in Majorca – it's *always* sunny in Majorca! Or saying the air on Mars is a bit thin – yeah, obvs! This is Glasgow, it rains. *A lot.*

But this wasn't your normal rain, the kind that gently pitter patters on your roof and drips off umbrellas. This was a full-blown monsoon, battering against the window of our flat in a wild, soggy torrent.

Usually I'm the one caught out in weather like that, because that's just my luck. I'm normally that drenched boy you pass in your warm car, soaked to the skin and looking like something a drowned rat would have a good laugh at. But on this occasion, I was lucky enough to be indoors. In the kitchen in fact, sitting at the table and looking out through the rain-blurred window.

"Something's not right," I said.

"What do you mean, boy?" asked Grandad, in an Indian accent fused with Glaswegian. Or, should I say, the ghost of my grandad, who sat beside me. Well, he didn't really sit, having no body to sit with, more floated in a sort of sitting position, which he often did to make himself feel less like what he was – an actual, real-life spectre. Not that it did any good. His face still had a green tinge, the kind you get with a bad case of seasickness, and he was completely see-through. To top it off he wore a Mackintosh raincoat with the collar turned up, a fedora hat and a pair of sunglasses. He looked ridiculous. Thankfully, nobody else could see him but me.

I leant forward and whispered, so that Mum couldn't hear. "Can't you take your coat and hat off? We're indoors."

"I am a ghost, Jayesh," he replied. "I can do what I want."

"Sorry? What's not right, dearie?" asked Mum, flouncing around the kitchen. She was cooking supper, though it looked more like she was doing some kind of weird modern dance. She had long flowing hair, and wore a long flowing scarf and long flowing dress, all of which were completely impractical for cooking, or indeed any form of human activity.

I stared down at the letter in my hands, which had dropped through our door out of the blue just a few weeks before. It was from Yummy Cola, the drinks company:

Mrs K Patel & Master J Patel

CONGRATULATIONS!!!

YOU HAVE WON A FABULOUS
WEEKEND BREAK AT A LUXURY
COUNTRY HOUSE HOTEL!

WE LOOK FORWARD
TO WELCOMING YOU AT
BRIGHTBURGH MANOR.

"The thing is, Mum, you said you never entered any competition for Yummy Cola."

She scoffed. "Why would I do that? Fizzy drinks are bad for your aura. And they make you burp."

That figured. My mum never drank anything that wasn't 100 per cent organic. Her idea of a refreshing beverage was a glass of carrot juice. If she wanted to push the boat out she might squeeze some honey in it, but that was about it. "Don't you get it?" I said. "If *you* didn't enter the competition, and *I* didn't enter the competition – how did we *win* the competition?"

"What?" she said, nonplussed.

"I mean, how did we win a competition we didn't put in for?"

Mum blinked, then shook her head and ladled something hot and steaming into a bowl, which I hoped against all hope was edible. "Jay, there's an age-old saying: 'Never look a gift horse in the mouth.'"

"She is right, son," said Grandad. "And besides, look at the brochure." He jabbed his finger at the photos of the hotel and the rooms, which looked quite plush. "Jacuzzis in every room!"

"So?" I whispered. "You can't even use a jacuzzi, you're dead."

"Do not rub it in," he said, offended.

"What did you say?" asked Mum.

It was so difficult always having two different conversations at once. I was constantly getting mixed up. Frankly, people were beginning to think I was weird. Apart from Mum, who was already a bit weird herself.

"There's another saying," I replied. "'If something looks too good to be true, then it probably is.'"

"Huh!" huffed Grandad. "Kids these days! They do not

know they are living. When I was your age, living in India, I would have walked twenty miles for a jacuzzi."

"Jacuzzis weren't even invented then!" I said, but then Mum looked at me quizzically, wondering what I was talking about. I shook my head. "Nothing! Look, it's *how* we won is the question."

"You think it is some kind of scam?" said Grandad.

"A scam?" I rubbed my chin. "Not sure. It's just odd, that's all."

Grandad was staring intently at the overhead light. His spooky eyeballs were twirling around in their sockets, watching a fly that was circling the lampshade. His face flashed with determination.

"That fly is annoying me. I am going to ghost-whack it!"

Grandad had ghostly powers. He could touch things, move things about, and even kick people. As for his spectral sneezes, they could blow up tiny whirlwinds. His special powers had helped me out of more than a few tight spots during our detective work. But lately he'd been suffering a crisis of confidence, a bit like a striker who could no longer score goals. He didn't believe he could do it.

Grandad floated higher, until his eyes were level with the bottom of the lampshade. He studied the fly's movements closely for a few seconds before slowly stretching out his arms.

"YAAAHH!" He slapped his hands shut on the fly.

Unfortunately, his hands just went right through each other. The fly didn't feel a thing, it just kept going round in circles. Grandad's face fell, and he sunk back down to the table like a deflated balloon. "I am a rubbish ghost!"

"A scam?" Mum snatched up a mallet and whacked the large gong that sat on the table. A gong that was about a foot away from my head. My eardrums quivered.

Then she yelled at the top of her voice:

"*DINN-ERRRR!*" which at least stopped my eardrums quivering, but made them wobble instead.

All this was for Granny's benefit, as she was hard of hearing.

Granny was a tiny terrier of a woman. And I mean tiny. She was once offered a part as one of Snow White's dwarves in the local panto. And she was shorter than some of the children playing the part. Lately she'd taken up karate. She burst through the door, dressed in a white karate outfit, with a bandana wrapped round her head.

She half-swaggered, half-waddled to the table. I blamed both the swagger and the waddle on the bodybuilding supplements she'd been taking. She said she wanted to look like she was in an action movie. I wasn't sure that a movie about karate grannies would be very successful.

"Ach, there's ma girl," said Grandad, grinning at her fondly. "Just as beautiful as the day I married her."

Granny suddenly snarled. A flash of white sleeve, and she lashed her arm out and karate-chopped the fly mid-air.

"HI-YAAA!"

The fly dropped with one pathetic final 'BUZZ', then thrashed around helplessly on its back on the kitchen floor.

Grandad's grin only got bigger. "What a woman!"

"Well," said Mum. "If it's a scam to get money out of us, dearie, then they chose the wrong people to mess with."

She wasn't wrong there. We didn't have any money to scam. Times were tight, especially since Dad disappeared off the face of the earth ten months previously.

Mum plonked the soup bowls in front of us. "Ta-daaaa!" she said, as if she'd just done a magic trick. "Kale, seaweed and turnip soup!"

I stared down at the contents of my bowl. My stomach turned. It looked like something you'd find at the bottom of a ditch. Smelt like it too.

Yes, times truly were tight.

I glanced at Granny. Her face was as white as her karate outfit. Her eye twitched at Mum. "Notice she disnae eat it!" she croaked.

Mum gave an airy flick of her hand. "I had a big lunch."

Grandad chortled. "For once, I am glad I am deid."

"Come on! Eat up!" Mum smiled. "We're off to the hotel early tomorrow morning. We're going to make a day of it!"

Granny caught my eye and nodded towards the pot plant near the kitchen table.

"See, Jayesh!" said Grandad. "The things your granny does for you."

He was right, because she was offering me her turn at using the plant pot to dispose of my dinner, which was amazingly generous given the food that was on offer.

I nodded thankfully, then waited until Mum's back was turned and tipped the contents of the bowl into the pot. The plant gulped it up.

SCHLLLUURRPPP!

A big rubbery thing, goodness knows how it survived with so much of Mum's cooking poured into it, but it did. In fact, it looked like it was thriving.

Granny winked at me. She adjusted her bandana, picked up her spoon and took a deep breath. I placed my hand on her shoulder and gave it a sympathetic squeeze. She reminded me of one of those kamikaze pilots from the Second World War, preparing to dive to their fiery (or in her case, soupy) death.

CHAPTER 2

The Dismal Day Out

Later that evening, I lay in bed turning the letter from Yummy Cola over in my fingers. The envelope had been stamped in Glasgow – nothing unusual in that. A standard window envelope with a self-sticking flap. There was a Yummy Cola logo stamped on the back which looked real enough, though you could easily knock that up on any computer.

"Maybe I'm just reading too much into it," I said.

"I think you are," replied Grandad, glowing ghostly green at the bottom of my bed, like the most annoying nightlight ever. "Did you not already phone the hotel? And they confirmed it was all OK."

"Yes."

He shrugged. "Well, there you are." Then he grinned. "One word: jacuzzis. They have jacuzzis." He laughed and tried to slap his thigh, except his hand just went right through. "Ugh." I suspected Grandad was looking forward to this trip more than I was.

I glanced up at the faded, yellowing poster above my bed, featuring my father wearing a turban and staring down ominously at a crystal ball. Dad was a stage magician called The Great Maharishi – before he disappeared, that is. Grandad and I had spent the past ten months searching for any clue of his whereabouts, not that it had helped. In the process, I'd turned into a detective, and Grandad was my somewhat annoying sidekick.

"Night, Grandad," I said, and switched off the light. I still wasn't entirely sure what he did to amuse himself when I was asleep. He couldn't read a book or a magazine, because he couldn't pick anything up. Sometimes, when he was at his most annoying, or I couldn't sleep because of his greeny glow, I would take him into the living room and put the TV on for him. But that was annoying too because the next morning all he would do was complain about what rubbish there was on the television these days. That night, I was so tired I left Grandad to make his own fun.

I dreamt about Dad, as I often did. He was on stage at the King's Theatre. He was in the middle of his favourite routine, which was called 'The Great Vanishing Act'. With a flourish of his cape, he shut himself inside a coffin-like box standing on stage. His assistant twirled the box round on its wheels, and then opened it again. The box was empty. The crowd gasped and applauded. Then a spotlight shone down on the wings, on the exact spot where Dad was meant to reappear. Except this time, he didn't. His assistant looked this way and that, her face suddenly worried. The audience looked confused. The applause died, as everyone fell into shocked silence.

Then, I was alone, standing right in the centre of Glasgow at St Enoch Square. Crowds of people were swarming by on either side, but I stood completely still, staring down the wide-open mouth of the subway station entrance. There was a subway ticket in my hand. I held it up and gazed at it. The ticket was issued at 12.01 pm on the day Dad disappeared. Where was he going? Was he involved in something that none of us knew anything about? I turned the ticket over. There on the back was a name, scrawled in blue ink in Dad's own hand:

Retain ticket for exit destination

Lyle Oaken

When I woke up the next morning, Grandad was gazing purposefully at that same subway ticket, which was pinned on my corkboard, together with the maps, newspaper cuttings, and any other bits of evidence I'd gathered. A web of orange string linked everything up.

The words 'LYLE OAKEN' were fainter now, after ten months, but they were still there.

"You're sure he's not dead?" I asked, rolling out of bed.

"Oh, good morning, Jayesh" he said. "No, I would know if he was up there." He pointed up at the ceiling. "And he is definitely not."

I yawned. "That subway ticket is still the only piece of real evidence we have." Which was very strange indeed. After all this time, there was virtually nothing to show why Dad had disappeared. How could someone have gone missing so publicly, so conspicuously, without even a trace? Unless he wanted to disappear, or needed to…

"I know, son," Grandad replied, "but do not worry. That is why I am here. I came back to help you find your father again. And we will."

After breakfast, I packed for the trip, stuffing some of my special detective equipment into my green Parka's deep pockets: my notebook, magnifying glass and my special plastic ruler, which was great for opening locks.

I found Grandad in the living room watching an old detective show on TV. "Have you seen this? It is called 'Miss Marple'. Everyone thinks she's just this sweet little old lady, but actually she is a master detective. Now, who does that remind you of?"

"I know," I said, because really she was a bit like me. Everyone thought I was just a (slightly weird) eleven year old, but I was actually a very talented super-sleuth in disguise.

"Me!" he said, jabbing his thumbs towards himself.

"What!?" I snorted. "Grandad, you couldn't solve a crime if it got up and gave you a haircut."

"What are you talking about? It is me who solves *all* the crimes in this family."

"Yeah, whatever. Now come on, it's time to go."

I hauled our suitcase down the stairs and stuffed it into Petal's rear end. 'Petal' was what Mum called our campervan, an aging relic, which was painted lime green. The inside was even worse, decked out in Indian fabrics and hanging beads. The beads especially were a nuisance – they kept swinging about and whacking us in the face whenever Mum hurtled round a corner. And she did a lot of hurtling.

"I would not be seen alive in this heap of junk," said Grandad, reluctantly floating into the back.

Granny jumped up into the passenger seat next to Mum, wearing a kimono and fanning herself with a copy of her

Shotokan Karate magazine. She was humming the theme tune to her favourite new movie, *Kung Fu Werewolves*. Me and Mum hadn't had the courage to tell Granny that her name wasn't actually on the invitation. We figured we'd leave that to the hotel, if they were brave enough, or mad enough, but I doubted it.

"Right," Mum sighed airily as she stuck the keys in the ignition, "we are now officially on holiday, so no argy-bargy." This sage advice was instantly ruined when she turned the ignition a couple of times and Petal's engine failed to start. Her face twisted into a fierce snarl and she punched the dashboard. "Come ONNNN, ya total pee stain!"

Eventually the engine choked into life, and we were off on our adventure. The hotel was at Loch Lomond, which wasn't far from Glasgow, but Mum insisted we keep stopping off on the way. The first stop was at a fair trade shop and café called Hippie-Chino. It was just her kind of place. She spent half an hour oohing and ahhing over everything before cleaning out her purse there, all so she could be the proud owner of some incense sticks, a packet of herbal tea and a soapstone sculpture of an elephant. After that, we had no money left to buy lunch.

"Don't worry, dearie, we'll eat when we get to the hotel. The food is all included, you know," she said.

The second stop-off was even worse. She brought the van to a screeching halt by the roadside, then kicked us out and shepherded us up a hillside. It turned out that the hillside was actually Ben Lomond, an actual mountain, and she wanted us to climb it. "It'll be good for the constitution," she declared. "Fresh air cleanses the aura."

We made a strange sight, traipsing up through the heather. Mum was wearing a pair of Dr. Martens that didn't match, together with a long dress, a flowing red scarf and a sun hat. The higher we climbed, the windier it got, so the scarf, the hat, the dress and her hair blew about all over the place. And she carried no supplies whatsoever: no water, food, energy bars, map, compass, nothing. The only thing she'd thought to bring along was a single rock, which she announced she was going to place on a cairn at the top. I at least had some provisions with me: a half-eaten, two-day-old bar of chocolate that I found lodged in my back pocket. And then there was Granny, dressed up like some kind of Japanese war-robot.

I huffed and puffed the whole way up the mountainside. Sweat was lashing off me, but not one bead of perspiration appeared on Granny's wrinkled brow. She would shoot off ahead of us, then turn and yell in her deep, croaky voice, "Come OAN, ya puddens!" Plonking herself down on a rock to wait for us, she would yawn, pull out her karate magazine and idly leaf through it.

A strange sight indeed. And that wasn't including the actual ghost that was trailing along behind us. Grandad thought the whole thing was hilarious. "Look at the state of you half-wits!"

It was alright for him. He could just float, which required no effort whatsoever.

Finally, at about four o'clock that afternoon, Mum had ticked off all of her 'must-see' stop-offs and we drove into Brightburgh village, where the hotel was situated. The village green was a pleasant, bustling place, fringed by cottages, shops and an inn, sloping gently down to the banks of Loch Lomond. The loch's waters were still and glassy, studded with wee wooded islands, and the banks on the other side rose up to the mountains.

Driving through the village, we came to another sign, one of those brown touristy ones.

"Here we are, dearies." Mum turned the campervan off the road, through an old stone gateway and then along a tidy gravel drive edged with trees.

Bhangra music was playing loudly on the van's radio, and Grandad was nodding and singing along with it at the top of his voice. He was waving his hands around and conducting an imaginary orchestra as he sang.

Mum was singing along too, shaking her head in time with the long stringy beads hanging down from the rearview mirror. Except she had no idea she was doing a duet.

The music stopped. Grandad smiled. "Ah, the old ones are always the best, eh, boy?"

Ahead, the trees opened out to wide, green fields and grazing cows. The grounds seemed to go on for miles.

"This is some back garden," I said.

"Up until a few years ago we would never have been allowed to see it," replied Mum. "This used to be a private estate. It was owned by an actual lord – Lord Brightburgh. He never allowed visitors. I checked it out on the internet."

At the head of the drive, about 250 metres away, stood a grand three-storey Victorian manor built of reddish sandstone and covered here and there with ivy. I kept thinking about this competition we'd won. A competition we'd never entered. And then I thought about my Dad and his disappearance. And the building we were headed to, which was really old. It was bound to be full of old bookcases, stairways and secret passageways. A building full of secrets to uncover. My detective nose was already twitching.

"So this lord, he *used* to own it. You mean he doesn't own it any more? What happened?"

"No, he went bankrupt a few years ago. He had to sell the whole estate. Then it opened as a hotel. He still lives here. They let him keep a wee cottage round the back."

Mum brought Petal crunching to a halt just outside the main entrance. A man stood at the top of the steps: thin, bald, with a droopy moustache and sunken shoulders, wearing a suit and tie. He looked miserable enough, but his face dropped even further when he clocked the van. I didn't blame him. I doubted vehicles like ours showed up very often in places like Brightburgh Manor.

"Er, hello," he said in a crisp English voice. "Can I help you?"

"Hullo," said Mum cheerily, as she raised one of her boots and kicked the car door shut. "The name's Patel. We're booked in."

"Oh, er, are you?" The man looked disappointed. Again, I didn't blame him. An eccentrically dressed woman, a scruffy eleven-year-old boy and a pensioner who looked like she'd just wandered off the set of a Japanese horror movie; we probably weren't the kind of clientele they were used to. And he didn't even know about the ghost. "Er, well, you'd better come in then. My name is Timothy Shand. I'm the hotel manager."

CHAPTER 3

The Awful Arrival

Shand led us into a big hall lined with antiques, high windows and dark panelled wood walls decorated with glassy-eyed mounted stags' heads. Velvet-covered sofas and chairs were clustered around, and there was a smell of burning logs from a great fireplace. A wide staircase led up to the first floor. Grandad suddenly drew up close to me. He was eyeing a suit of armour standing stiffly at the other side of the hall.

"Hey, I do not like that guy there," he said in a nervous voice.

"It's only a suit of armour."

"There is still a dead guy in it. Look…" Grandad blinked his eyes, which was always a bad sign. It meant that I could now see everything he could see. Not very nice things. Specifically, all the ghosts!

A face was staring out at me from the helmet visor. I say a face, it was more like a gruesome, rotting skull with eyes. And when I say eyes I mean *eye*, because only one of them was remotely where it should be, in a socket. The other was dangling out.

"You! YOU!" the spectre growled. "You arrant knave, cometh here whilst I smite you!" The ghost's dangly eyeball swung precariously as he spoke.

"Huh!" said Grandad. "Fat chance of you smiting anyone in your condition."

"Grandad, please!" I said, not wanting to witness any more of their 'argy-bargy' as Mum would call it.

Grandad blinked again, and the gruesome face was gone.

Since Grandad came back I've learnt that there are ghosts everywhere; they're on the streets, they're in shops, in houses and schools. They walk among us. It's just that most of us can't see them (so be careful where you sit).

A hotel porter wearing a smart black jacket appeared. He picked up a leather case belonging to an old lady with a walking stick who seemed to have just checked in. The initials 'VH' were stitched into the side of her expensive-looking luggage.

"Follow me, Mrs Hackenbottom," said the porter in a Polish accent, before bounding up the stairs two at a time. He turned to wait for the old lady, a sheen of sweat glistening on his forehead.

"I shall be right with you," warbled the woman, unhitching her cane from the crook of her elbow. "*Hacken*? *Bottom*? Did you hear that?" Grandad burst out laughing, making a hacking motion with his hand against his ghostly bum. "Hackenbottom!"

The lady hobbled painfully slowly towards the first step.

Grandad cupped his hand next to his mouth, calling out to the porter. "You are going to be waiting a while there, mate!"

The porter waited patiently at the top of the stairs for the elderly guest, but her expensive suitcase must have weighed a ton – the handles slipped in the porter's sweaty hands and hit the floor with a thump.

"My case!" the old woman cried. Then, to our surprise, she bounded up the steps.

"Huh! She is sprightlier than I thought," said Grandad.

"She'd make a nice girlfriend for you," I smirked.

Grandad held up his finger at me. "Hey, your granny, the love of my life – and after-life – is right here!"

And so she was, doing fist pump exercises into a full-length mirror a short distance away, making fierce snarling noises with every tenth punch. So fierce it sounded a bit like someone throwing up.

There was a couple in front of us at the reception desk, a man and a woman. The man wore chinos, tan loafers and a jumper wrapped round his shoulders. He laughed smugly and swept his hand through his mane of wavy hair."Oh, darling, really!" I heard him say.

The woman did a lot of smug laughing too, tossing her curly black hair back and forward. "Yes, DAAAH-LING!" she brayed, then they turned and clocked me, standing there in my jeans, and Mum in her flowy dress and muddy

Dr. Martens. They looked us up and down and attempted to smother another laugh.

The couple moved off, and Mum, who hadn't even noticed, stepped forward and dangled the letter in Shand's face, making him jerk. "We're the Yummy Cola competition winners!" she declared.

He reluctantly took the sheet of paper from her, inspected it, then nodded. "Ah."

Shand reached behind the reception desk, pulled out a card and pushed it towards Mum. "Can you fill out this registration card, please, madam?"

"Why, of course I can, my good man," she replied in her finest fake posh voice. Then she put on a weird high-pitched fake laugh, which was quite embarrassing.

Mum picked up the pen and started filling in the card, humming some tune that was in her head. At that point a lady appeared from the office door marked **PRIVATE** on the other side of reception. Her hair looked like a giant white blancmange perched on top of her head. She had a tiny scrunched up mouth and she was plastered in garish makeup. The woman looked Mum over like she was inspecting a mouse she'd caught in a mousetrap. Then she took in Granny, who'd finished her fist pumps and was now standing with her arms folded up in her kimono sleeves, looking like some kind of mystical troll. Finally, she turned her eyes on me and that seemed to tip her over the edge. She wrinkled her nose in disgust and screwed her mouth up, as if she was sucking on a particularly sour lemon.

I tried to smile back at her, but it only made her face drop and her mouth scrunch up even more, until she looked like something from a horror movie.

Grandad whistled through his teeth. "I would not like to meet her on a dark night."

Shand glanced at the woman and caught the expression. "These are guests," he explained, before turning back to us with a smile that didn't reach his eyes. "This is my wife, Mrs Shand."

She glared at him, as if insulted, and spoke in a screechy, snobby voice. "Guests?! May I speak with you, Timothy?"

"Certainly, dear," said Shand with a gulp.

They stepped into an office behind the reception desk. The man's shoulders drooped further, and his moustache even further still. Mrs Shand slammed the door shut. I heard them arguing under their voices. About us.

"I told you," she squeaked. "We need a better class of person at this hotel. No riff-raff."

"I know that, dear," he murmured. "But I'm afraid we need every penny we can get!"

A slight movement behind the desk caught my eye. I'd been so distracted by Shand and his wife's (now quite loud) argument that I hadn't spotted a woman of about nineteen sitting at the computer. Her hair was dyed black, and she was wearing black eyeliner, black lipstick and black clothes. All of this was in sharp contrast to her chalk-white face, on which sat a long and slightly aquiline nose. Her lips were curled up in a kind of snarl,

and there was a fierce and icy look in her blue eyes.
Her name badge said

Lucy

"Phew! There's another one I would not like to bump
into on a dark night," commented Grandad.

The girl turned her head to listen to Mr and Mrs
Shand's argument. Then she tutted, sighed angrily and
shook her head. She glanced at me out of the side of her
eye as she turned back to the screen, but her look went
straight through me. I got that a lot. No one thinks you're
worth noticing when you're only eleven. Quite often, it's
their biggest mistake. And my biggest advantage.

Shand emerged from the office, his face flushed, as
Mum finished filling in the card and handed it to him.
She hadn't heard any of the conversation, but then Mum
was on another planet for most of the time. She once
walked past me in the street without noticing. "There you
go," she beamed. "I drew you a wee flower on it as well."

Shand looked at the card, together with the doodle Mum
had scrawled on it, with more than an ounce of disdain.

"I see. Thank you, madam. Would you like our porter,
Arek to get your bags?" He gestured towards the man
in the black uniform who'd just made it back down the
stairs after showing the old lady to her room. Young and
thin with a nest of brown hair and a mole on his upper

lip, he seemed a little out of breath. And still very sweaty.

"No, do not do that!" said Grandad, waving his arms. "You will have to tip the guy. They expect dosh, these hotel porters."

"No thanks," replied Mum, grinning at me. "Why get a porter to humph my bags around when I have a perfectly good son?"

"No, really, it's fine, I will get it," said the porter, which was probably the nicest thing anyone had said to me all day. As he leant forward to pick up Granny's bag, her wrist flicked up, barring the way. He stared at her clenched fist, her knuckles white and bony, then at her narrowed, twitching eyes.

"Ah'll get it!" she croaked, like a demonically possessed doll.

He looked somewhat terrified. And I didn't blame him. I was somewhat terrified as well, and she was my granny.

The porter backed away, hands up, like someone retreating from a chance encounter with a bear in the woods. All of which left Granny to lug her own case, and me to grapple with Mum's.

"Very well," said Shand. "Er, this way."

He led us towards the stairs, where there was a display cabinet set into the wall. It was full of trophies and china vases, but a large silver bell took pride of place. It struck me as a bit strange why anyone would want to put a bell on display, so I stopped to give it a closer look.

"Bells," said Grandad. "Pff. Yawn-amundo."

Grandad always comes out with stuff like that. I think it's old-fashioned slang from when he was alive. Basically you just stick '-amundo' on the end of words. It's pretty lame (-amundo).

Shand stopped, noticing my interest in the display.

"That, young man, is the famous Brightburgh silver bell."

Grandad's face screwed up. "Famous? Why have I not heard of it?"

"It dates back to 1134 AD, when it was gifted to Lord Brightburgh's family by King David I. Like all of Lord Brightburgh's possessions, it is now owned by the hotel."

"So it's yours?" I asked.

He see-sawed his head slightly from side to side. "Sort of, but it has protected status, so we can't sell it."

"Must be worth a few bob, though?" I added.

"Indeed. It is priceless," said Shand.

Grandad's ears always pricked up when money got mentioned.

"How much? Ask him how much," he said. 'Antiques Roadshow' was his favourite programme, although compared with most things *he* was the antique.

"'Priceless', he said. There is no price," I replied to Grandad through gritted teeth.

Grandad tried to fold his arms, disappointed, but they just went through each other. I turned back to Shand, who was staring at me oddly.

"So, are you not scared it'll get nicked then?" I asked him.

Shand smiled smugly. "Impossible. It's alarmed."

In my experience there was no such thing as impossible. I should know, my own grandad had come back from the dead to haunt me.

CHAPTER 4

The Ghostly Jacuzzi

Shand led us up the winding staircase. The red-carpeted hallway on the first floor was lined with oil paintings and stone busts of long-dead posh people on plinths. He eventually stopped outside a carved oak door. He turned the handle and raised an eyebrow at Mum.

"Madam, this one is yours."

He pushed the door open to reveal a vast room with large windows and a four-poster bed.

"Wow! Oh, WOW!" Mum sprinted inside, dived into the air and then belly-flopped on the mattress. "YIPPEE!" she yelped, bouncing up and down on the bed.

DOIING! DOIING! DOIING! DOIING!

"And your room is just through the connecting door there." Shand pointed me towards a door at the other end of Mum's room. Then he glanced questioningly at Granny. "It's a room for one."

Granny stared him down, her eye twitching furiously,

and then growled. Shand shrunk away. "Er, I'll leave you to make your own arrangements."

That meant the single room that was supposed to be for me, and me alone, was also going to be Granny's room. Oh, and Grandad's too. I was stuck with the two of them.

Shand left us, closing the door behind him. I wandered into my room to find it was just as posh as Mum's. Granny gazed around, unimpressed. Her karate instructor preached simplicity as the path to enlightenment, so at home she'd dispensed with her proper bed and now slept on a bamboo mat on the floor. She'd brought the mat with her, and pulled it out of her bag, whipping it in the air with the same kind of flourish as a bullfighter flicking his cape, before laying it in the corner.

Granny nodded, satisfied, then turned and left.

Mum hovered at the connecting door, looking around and nodding at my room. "Hmm, nice." She grasped the door knob. "Well, I'll leave you to it. I'm going to meditate." Mum gave a smile, then yanked the door shut behind her.

I wasted no time. I felt round the bedroom walls, tapping them firmly with my fingers.

"What are you doing?" asked Grandad.

"Seeing if the walls are hollow." My detective instincts were tingling. I wanted to find out if there were any secret passageways leading to my room. I knew for a fact that we hadn't entered the competition, which meant there was a good chance we'd been brought here for a reason – but why? I intended to find out.

I soon came to a spot where the wall sounded different. Hollow.

"Do me a favour, Grandad," I said. "Stick your head through there."

"What? No!"

"Just to see," I wheedled. "Come on, you're a ghost. It can't hurt you."

He waved his hands about. "No, no, no, nothing doing. I hate going through walls."

"Please, Grandad. I'm not asking you to go straight through it. Just peek inside. A quick peek, that's all."

Grandad sighed. "Fine."

He took a deep breath, then cautiously poked his head inside the wall. "Yuck! I really do hate this!" The back of his behatted head disappeared, followed by his shoulders, arms and most of his back. Only his rear end was sticking out on my side. I fleetingly wished I could give it a little kick, but my foot would have gone straight through.

"Jayesh?" I heard his muffled voice calling from the other side.

There was a door nearby, which I flung open. I found myself staring out into the hallway. Aha! So my room had its own door. That was good; it meant I could get out and snoop without having to go through Mum's room. Looking round, I realised that the wall sounded hollow because it was indeed thinner there than at any other part. It was an alcove, containing a statue of a beautiful woman dressed in a toga. A beautiful woman who now had Grandad's confused face instead of her own.

"This feels weird," he said. "But I look rather good in a dress, don't you think?"

Returning to the room, I peered out of the window, trying to get my bearings. The room looked down on to a large walled garden, full of manicured lawns and tinkling fountains. Granny was there, standing in the middle of an oversized garden chessboard, viciously karate-kicking the chess pieces to the ground.

My bathroom was huge. There, I set eyes on the hugest bathtub I'd ever seen. A real live jacuzzi. I'd never been in a jacuzzi before. Grandad was right. This was exciting! While I was dying to snoop around a bit more, it had been a long day. "Grandad," I called out. "I'm going to have a jacuzzi." I turned on the taps and watched them scoosh out water. Grandad didn't reply. I went back into the room, but he wasn't there. Had he gone for a walk – or rather, a float? Perhaps he'd gone to find Granny. Or maybe he was still out in the hallway, finding his inner Greek goddess. I peeked through the door's spy hole, but he wasn't out there either.

"Yes! Freedom at last!" I did a lap of honour round the room.

But when I went back into the bathroom to turn off the taps, I discovered Grandad hadn't gone for a float after all. He was lying in the bath. My bath.

"Uch, Grandad!"

"What was that you were shouting there, boy?" He was fully clothed, complete with his Mackintosh coat, hat and sunglasses. He slouched back, his arms stretched out along the bath rim, just as the bath went into jacuzzi mode.

"Ahhhhhh!"

"Hey, that bath was for me," I protested.

"Well, it is mine now, son," he replied with a satisfied smile.

"That's not fair, you can't even enjoy it." I slumped down on the toilet seat.

Grandad took off his shades, and a strange wistful look came into his eyes. "You know, I really miss having baths. Baths are brilliant. It really is no fun, this ghost business."

"Are you kidding?" I replied, hoping to try and persuade him to get out. "Look at all the cool stuff you get to do. I mean, I know you don't like walking through walls, but what about frightening people... and moving stuff around?"

"Jayesh, son, you know fine well I am rubbish at moving stuff around." He rose up out of the bath, then hovered, looking around the room. He fixed his eyes on a tube of toothpaste that was lying by the sink "Watch this. I'm going to try and lift it up." He floated over and tried to wrap his hands around it. He concentrated hard. After a moment, his face started turning red – well, a greenish kind of red – and his eyes bulged out of their sockets. But the tube didn't move. He gritted his teeth and veins burst out of his forehead. Eventually, the tube started to shake violently.

"You're getting somewhere," I cried. "Keep trying!"

Suddenly, the lid of the tube exploded off and toothpaste squirted all over the bathroom.

Grandad cheered. "Hey, brilliant! Did you see that? Maybe I am not so bad after all."

"Yeah, Grandad, cosmic!" I sighed, knowing I would be the one who had to clean it all up.

After I'd tidied up Grandad's show of spectral strength and got washed and changed, I joined up with Mum, who'd been having a much more relaxing time of it in her own room, making angel shapes on top of the bed.

She shrugged. "Who cares that we never even entered a silly competition? Look at this place!" She took the opportunity to belly-flop on the springy mattress once again, yelping almost as much as she did the first time.

"Like she said, never look a gift horse in the mouth." Grandad floated in behind me.

"Hmm," I mused. "But what if the gift horse is carrying a baseball bat behind its back?"

With that, we headed downstairs for dinner.

CHAPTER 5

The Penne Problem

Mr and Mrs Shand were standing at the door of the dining room. He was dressed in a tuxedo, she was wearing an evening dress. She surveyed my crumpled jumper and jeans in horror, and her look didn't improve as she took in the rest of my family. Mum hadn't changed either, and Granny was still sporting her karate outfit. Mr Shand reluctantly showed us to a table.

The dining room was busy. The person sitting nearest to our table was a man in his late thirties.

"Here you are, Mr Starkey," said the waiter as he placed a bowl of soup on the man's table. Starkey looked like an accountant or a lawyer. He had that grey look, the look of a man drained of life by decades of boring work. As is turned out, Mr Starkey would be feeling a lot more drained in a few minutes' time.

A decrepit old lady was standing at his table, leaning over her walking stick and craning her head towards him. I realised it was the same old woman we'd seen in the reception earlier that day.

She seemed to be one of those old busybody types.

You know, the kind that likes to annoy people by inflicting long, slow conversations on them.

"Oh, what are you having, Mr Starkey?" she droned.

"Chicken noodle soup, Mrs Hackenbottom."

"The soup, ah, how lovely. I had chicken noodle soup once. I was violently ill."

Starkey grimaced. He was trying to be polite, but it was clear he just wanted this woman to go away, and I didn't blame him.

We sat down and picked up our menus. Grandad of course didn't have a menu, or a seat. He was floating behind me, peering over my shoulder.

"Let me see! Let me see!"

I snatched the leather-bound menu away from him. "You can't even eat."

"That is a mean thing to say!"

My heart sank as the old woman turned to our table. Mum's face was buried in her menu, and I hid behind mine, but it didn't stop her. She squeezed Mum's forearm.

"Just saying hello, dear. I'm Vera Hackenbottom."

Mum loved meeting people. Even old, annoying ones. "It's awful nice of you to say hello, Vera," she said, beaming.

"Pff!" said Grandad. "Busybottom, more like!"

The old lady flashed a set of grey teeth at Granny. "And you too, dear."

Granny just glared at her, the way a hungry eagle might glare at a shrew that had the misfortune to pitch up inside its nest.

Mrs Hackenbottom gestured her cane towards a table at the window, which was set for one. "I'm just over there if you need me." She tottered away with her walking stick.

"Ha! Need her? For what?" scoffed Grandad. "Boring people to death?"

Mum grinned and cocked her head to one side. "Uch, that was nice, wasn't it? What a nice wee lady."

Grandad tried to snatch the menu from me, forgetting once again that he couldn't snatch anything if his life, or even his death, depended on it.

"Ach!" he protested. "Tell her not to order penne pasta. I will be sick if she has penne pasta. I HATE penne pasta."

"There's not even penne pasta on the menu," I said.

"See, that's what I was looking for, if you'd just let me," he huffed.

"Oh, do you want penne pasta?" Mum asked.

I shook my head, firmly enough, I thought.

"NO!" cried Grandad.

"I can ask." Mum turned towards the waiter.

"I don't want penne pasta," I said, starting to get annoyed. Why did every conversation in my family have to go like this?

"Oh, all your talking about it has put me in the notion." She waved a finger at the waiter. "Excuse me."

The waiter, who was wearing a smart waistcoat, came rushing over. There were beads of sweat on his brow, which was familiar. So was the nest of brown hair, and the mole on his upper lip. We'd seen this man before, just in a different uniform. Mum noticed too, as she waggled her finger at him, quizzically. "Eh… wait, are you not the porter?"

"That is my brother, Arek," he replied in a curt Polish accent. "He carries suitcases. I'm Parek, the waiter."

"Arek and Parek… Well, that is not confusing at all," huffed Grandad, still in a mood.

"Do you have penne pasta?" Mum asked the waiter.

"Yes, madam," he replied.

"Oh, goodie. Penne pasta for me, then." She closed her menu with a satisfied smile.

"I'll have the chicken burger," I said. "But can I have it fast?" I was starving.

"Uh!" Grandad grunted. "I LOVE chicken burgers. It really is RUBBISH being a ghost."

"And you, madam?" The waiter turned to Granny.

"*Suki yaki*," Granny barked.

"Pardon?"

"*SUKI YAKI!*" she barked even louder, sounding like a sea lion with a bad case of bronchitis.

"Yes, I heard," he said politely. "But who or what is *suki yaki*?"

Granny rose from her seat, eyeing him venomously, and rolled up her sleeves. All of which meant she was probably about to give him a doing. I defused the situation with a cough.

"Let me explain the recipe," I said. "Take a can of sardines…"

"Right..." He frantically scribbled in his pad.

"Open it, turn it upside down, dump it into a bowl, then mash it up, and finally – and this is the pièce de résistance – crumble in some cream crackers."

"That's it?" The waiter looked confused. "That's what she wants to eat?"

"Yup."

Granny claimed that this dish, if you could call it that, was traditional Japanese cuisine, though I'd be surprised if even the cats in Japan would eat it. She started eating it when she took up karate. It was her *sensei's* (her karate instructor's) favourite meal. Having said that, her *sensei's* previous job was working in the kitchens at HM Barlinnie prison.

I turned to Grandad while Granny and Mum finished their order. "Why do you hate penne pasta so much?"

"I saw a seagull regurgitate some once," he replied. "And then its chick gobbled it up. It was revolting."

I nodded. "Fair enough." My family is so weird. "But look, she's ordered it now, you've brought this on yourself. You're the one who mentioned it."

Grandad was furious. He tried stomping his feet, but it didn't really work given that he had no real feet to stomp. "I am not stopping here if she is going to be eating penne pasta."

"Off you go then." I fluttered my fingers at the door. This caught Mum's attention. She looked at me for a second, before realising that I hadn't been talking to her.

She shook her head and turned back to the waiter. It was a wonder she didn't think I was mad.

"I'm sitting with somebody else," said Grandad. "That man there." There was an empty seat pulled out at Starkey's table and he made a point of sitting down on it, even though, as a ghost, he couldn't really sit. Starkey had his napkin tucked into the neck of his shirt and was quietly eating his chicken noodle soup, completely unaware he was now dining with the deceased.

Grandad looked over at me and made a face, so I made one back. Unfortunately, this was caught by Mr Shand, who'd come into the dining room to check on his guests. All he saw was me gurning into thin air. Unsurprisingly, he looked horrified, then he shook his head and left.

"Waiter! Waiter!" Mrs Hackenbottom called insistently from her table by the window, rubbing her arms. "Please ask somebody to close the windows. It's terribly cold."

The waiter sighed, and another drip of sweat appeared on his brow. "Yes, right away." He rushed off, muttering under his breath.

"Sorry dear, I'm so frail!" she called after him, cradling her arms.

Grandad scoffed at me, then turned to Starkey. "Nice hotel, eh?"

Starkey suddenly started sniffing the air. "Ewww! What's that funny smell?" Then he screwed up his face. "And what's that awful taste?"

"Eh?" Grandad looked affronted. He sniffed his own ghostly armpits. "Well, it is not me."

Starkey leapt to his feet. His face turned bright purple and his lips even purpler. His eyes bulged and his hands flew to his throat. For a brief second, I thought he was doing some kind of weird dance routine. Grandad stared at him like he was crazy.

There was a colossal choke, then Starkey's mouth started frothing. He slumped back down onto his seat, and his face fell forward into his soup...

PLOP

The whole restaurant stopped. Many, for one hushed, stunned moment, thought it was a practical joke or one of those weird theatre dining experiences. But then gasps of shock went up from the other diners, some of whom tossed their napkins aside and ran to Mr Starkey's table as they realised he wasn't moving.

Grandad jumped to his feet and held up his hands. "It was not me! It was not me!"

The first person to reach Starkey was the well-groomed posh man who had laughed at us in reception earlier. He'd been dining in the far corner with his glamorous lady friend, who had changed into an emerald green evening dress for dinner. The man carefully retrieved Starkey's face from the soup and took his pulse.

He shared a look with his companion, then slowly shook his head, just as Mr Shand ran into the dining room.

"I think he's dead."

CHAPTER 6

The Deadly Soup

The lady in the green dress nudged her friend out of the way. "I used to be a nurse." She snatched a napkin and wiped Starkey's face clean of the pieces of soupy chicken and bits of noodles, trying to try find a pulse in his neck, but it was no use.

"Carry Mr Starkey to the office," whispered a pale-looking Shand to the waiter.

"Has he really kicked the bucket?" asked Grandad, as the waiter dragged Starkey unceremoniously by the feet out of the dining room. The lady went with him, stopping only to snatch up a green snakeskin diary that was sitting on her table.

"Well, he doesn't look too healthy," I replied.

Everyone was in shock. A few of the diners rushed out, whimpering into their napkins. Another was trying to explain what was happening to a bunch of German men who were here on a golfing holiday. They didn't speak a word of English, and I don't think they understood the explanation, because they were nodding, smiling and clapping their hands. "Ya! YA!" They seemed to think this was all part of some sort of evening entertainment.

As for Mrs Hackenbottom, she barely looked up from her chicken Balmoral. "You know what I think," she said in her loud, grating voice. She swirled a mouthful of haggis around, spitting little bits of it out of the side of her mouth as she spoke.

"What?" I said, still shocked.

"There's something wrong with the food. It's food poisoning."

Shand came back in the room. He heard her and bridled, "Oh, please, Mrs Hackenbottom."

One of the diners at another table heard her too. He stood up and signalled Shand. "Get our bill please, we're leaving."

"Food poisoning? Yes, us too," said another couple.

"*Food poisoning!*" repeated the old lady, even louder this time.

Shand's face went from white to red. "PLEASE! Mrs Hackenbottom!" He turned to the other diners, who were starting to crowd round. "Please, everyone, we don't know what happened to Mr Starkey yet..."

The other diners seemed to be voting with their feet. The dining room was clearing out.

"Pff!" said Grandad, staring at Mrs Hackenbottom. "If she thinks there is something wrong with the food, then why is she eating it? Ask her, Jayesh."

"Yeah, good point." I turned to her. "Why are you eating the food, then, if you think it's poisoned?"

The old lady grinned at me, scooping up another fork

load of chicken, haggis and peas. "Ha! I'm far too old to care, young man."

"Ach" She's just a stirrer." Grandad shook his head. "A stirry old bat. That's what she is. She's enjoying this."

We heard a sudden, loud clattering from the kitchen followed by an angry cry.

"WHaTT?!"

The service door flew open and a large man in chef's whites and hat appeared, silhouetted against the stark kitchen lights. He had a waxed black moustache, a wild, ferocious glare in his eye and he was brandishing a potato peeler. "Who said 'food poisoning'? he growled in a foreign accent I couldn't place. He glared at the diners as they scurried past him, before settling on the smartly dressed man who'd taken Starkey's pulse. "YOU!"

The chef gripped the man's wrist with his mighty fist. "What are YOU doing here?"

"What do you mean? Get your hand off me!" replied the man, his mane of hair waving about as the chef shook him violently.

The two of them struggled, before Shand intervened. "Gentlemen, please! What is this about?"

The chef jabbed his potato peeler at the man. "Don't you know who he is? He is Benedict Ravensbury, the restaurant critic."

"So what if I am?" replied Ravensbury.

"He gave me a bad review once," spat the chef. "He said

my *bündner nusstorte* had a soggy bottom. How dare you show your face in my restaurant!"

Ravensbury swiped his hand. "That was years ago. Anyway, I'm not here on business. My friend Chase and I just came up for a spot of hill walking."

Shand fidgeted and tried to get them to lower their voices. "Shh, please, calm down."

But the chef was in no mood to be shushed. He tossed his potato peeler into his other hand, like an assassin juggling his dagger, then jabbed at Ravensbury with his thick, sausagey forefinger. "Your problem is you do not understand your job. Swiss cuisine is hugely diverse. After all..." He looked round at everyone, turning on a well-meaning smile and appealing for support. "Many people say the Swiss fondue is a lost art."

Parek, the waiter, entered and rolled his eyes. "Oh, is he on about Swiss food again?"

Now the chef turned on him. "YOU! What did you say?"

"Nothing. Your food is lovely," replied the waiter.

"I heard you! You always criticize my food. You said my venison was like eating shoe leather. I heard you!"

"Yes, I apologise for that..." said the waiter.

"Good!" said the chef.

"To *shoe leather*!" The waiter went on. "Your venison was even worse. It was like gnawing on a shipyard worker's old boots"

The chef's face went scarlet, and he exploded.

"DaHHHH!" He chased the waiter out of the room, waving his potato peeler like a sword.

"Well, I'm not leaving the dining room, not 'til I'm finished," said Mrs Hackenbottom. She leaned over in my direction and muttered, "They're trying to sell this place, you know."

"Really?" I acted surprised, even though it had been obvious from the Shands' overheard argument on our arrival that they were having financial problems.

"Oh, yes. They're broke, Shand and his wife."

"I bet this place is cursed." Grandad looked around the room ominously.

Mrs Hackenbottom leaned even closer, and whispered, "I mean, who'd want to buy it now, eh?"

"She is not wrong there," said Grandad. "Diners dropping in their soup. Crazy chefs running about waving potato peelers. I do not think I would buy it."

The dining room was empty, apart from us and Mrs Hackenbottom. Oh, and the German golfers, who'd broken into some kind of jolly sing-song, and were all smiles and rosy cheeks, swaying from side to side in unison. They had absolutely no idea what was going on. We hung about for a bit, waiting to see if anything else might happen, and listening to the old lady swill food around her mouth. I was so hungry. I was hoping the chef would calm down enough to make me a chicken burger, but after a while it seemed like my luck was out.

"We may as well go, I'm not going to get fed," I said.

"OK, dearie," said Mum.

"It beats hanging about here with this old trout," huffed Grandad.

I got up from my seat and stared down at the remains of Starkey's soup, which had spilled over the tablecloth and the floor. Having evaded the chef, Parek the waiter came rushing in with a cloth to wipe it all up. Probably, Starkey had choked, or suffered a heart attack or something.

Probably.

Then I thought about the strange way he'd keeled over, the look on his face, the frothing of his lips. Yummy Cola had brought us here, I thought, perhaps for good reason. Was something dark and mysterious afoot? And if so, what did it have to do with me?

CHAPTER 7

The Soupy Suspects

The ambulance soon arrived and the paramedics rushed into the hotel foyer. Starkey had been carried into the office behind the reception desk, and the paramedics trooped inside with a stretcher.

"You're too late! You're too late!" joked Grandad.

"That's not even funny, Grandad!" I hissed out of the side of my mouth.

"Ach!" He swiped his hand. "I am allowed to joke, I am the one that's deid after all." He waved a finger at me. "Death is not the end, you know that."

He was right. In Grandad's case it was just the start of a very active and annoying afterlife.

"I'm sending out positive thoughts for the poor man," said Mum. She closed her eyes and clasped her hands together in meditation. A vacant, silly sort of grin appeared on her face, the kind someone gets when they ease themselves into a nice hot bath.

Most of the people from the dining room were gathered in the reception, and the commotion was loud enough that I didn't think anybody would notice me turning again to talk with Grandad. "Do *you* think it was food poisoning?"

"You mean the normal, bacterial kind? No way," he replied. "Plenty of other people had the soup, and it didn't affect them. Anyway, food poisoning, with bacteria and that, takes much longer to kick in."

"Are you sure?"

"Oh, I should know, I used to own a restaurant. Loads of my customers came down with food poisoning, but it was always after they left." He nodded his head knowledgably.

Something smelt off to me, and I wasn't talking about the food. "Did you see the way he was acting, his face? And the frothing at the mouth? And he was complaining about a funny taste and smell." It was the other sort of poisoning that I was thinking of. The deliberate, deadly kind. "Lots of actual poisons do have a funny smell. Cyanide, for example, smells of bitter almonds."

"You think someone poisoned the food on purpose?" Grandad asked.

"Yes, it's possible. If I only knew what the funny smell was like..."

Grandad shrugged. "I can't smell, unfortunately. Otherwise I could have told you. And you can't smell it now either, because it's all been mopped up."

A waft of air from the open front door brought the arrival of a pair of hunting beagles, sniffing around and wagging their tails, followed by heavy footsteps.

A tall man wearing a tweed jacket, red cords and brown

brogues strode into the lobby. He was an older man with neat greying hair, but still had the swagger and bearing of someone much younger.

His voice boomed through the hall. "What the ruddy nora is going on? Why is there an ambulance blocking my drive?"

The porter, Arek was sweating at the foot of the stairs. "A man was taken ill, sir," he said.

The man glared at him for a moment, his mouth twisted to one side and one eye screwed up, like a pirate captain ogling his slovenly crew. "In that case, I suppose I'll have to wait." He strode round the hall like he owned the place.

"That's him," whispered Mum, taking a break from her meditation. The man stopped, leaned over the display case and scrutinised the silver bell.

"Who?" I asked.

"The guy I told you about, Lord Brightburgh. The guy who went bust and lost the whole estate."

"Oh." I watched as he wandered over in our direction, nodding at Mum.

"Good evening."

"Oh, hello." Mum's smile was even wider than usual, and her cheeks went red. "Goodness me, an actual lord! Pleased to meet you."

Granny narrowed her eyes and bowed, like he was an opponent at a karate tournament.

Up close, he had a slightly hooked nose and icy blue eyes. His eyebrows seemed to have a life of their own.

"Disgraceful, what they've done to this place," he barked.

He stopped at the reception desk and cast his eye round some of the gathered crowd, just as the paramedics carried the stretcher out of the office. Starkey was in a body bag, which had been partially zipped closed.

Everyone else was staring at Starkey's disappearing corpse, but I couldn't help but notice how Lord Brightburgh's face changed. It went pale. Ghostly pale. Mr Shand came rushing out of the dining room, wringing his hands. "Oh, Lord Brightburgh, good evening."

The lord hesitated for a moment. "Good evening, Shand," he said eventually. "Spot of bad luck, eh?"

"One of our guests was taken ill at dinner."

"I see." Lord Brightburgh's eyes flitted back across the room, while Shand fussed around the reception desk.

The lord rubbed his chin. "Er, I say, Shand, could I ask for some help from one of your people, just to get my bags in the car. As soon as that ambulance moves, that is. I'm off to Edinburgh for the night."

"Oh," said Shand absently. "Er, yes, of course. Arek was here a minute ago." He called over to the receptionist with the black hair and permanent scowl. She was wielding a long pole to forcefully shut the lobby's high windows. "Lucy, where's Arek gone?"

Lucy stacked the pole in a corner. "He just went through the back," she said tersely, rolling up her sleeves. "I'll do it. I'm stronger than I look." She stomped out alongside Lord Brightburgh and his dogs.

Meanwhile I clocked a familiar figure treading discreetly up the stairs, looking over her shoulder to see if she was being watched. It was Ravensbury's friend, Chase, carrying her green snakeskin diary under her arm.

"She's got suspicious written all over her. What's she up to?" I said.

"Shall I go after her?" asked Grandad.

"No, we both will." I slipped away from Mum and Granny, and sprang quietly up the stairs behind her.

Tiptoeing down the hall past our rooms, I halted at the corner and peeked around it. Grandad's glowing green face poked out from behind mine. Together, we watched Chase stop outside a door halfway along the corridor. She glanced over her shoulder again, and I whipped my head back under cover before she had a chance to spot me.

I nodded Grandad forward. The best thing about a ghost sidekick was having an invisible pair of eyes.

"Leave it to me." He floated into the middle of the corridor. "She has got her credit card out," he called back. "She is poking it into the side of the door and jiggling it about." He floated towards her, out of view, as the jiggling continued. "Her surname is Whitton by the way. It says so on her bank card," he added.

Wow, that was actually quite useful, I thought. Grandad was getting better at detective work.

I could hear the click as the door unlocked. "She's in," said Grandad.

That was fast, I thought, she must have sprung a lock

before. This woman wasn't your average hotel guest, but then, neither was I. I could have had that lock open in half the time using my bendy plastic ruler. "The coast is clear."

"Whose room is it?" I mouthed at Grandad as I crept closer to the door. I nodded him forward again. "Look inside."

Grandad huffed. "Aw, not again. I HATE going through stuff."

"This is important!" I hissed.

He sighed loudly, then took a deep breath and plunged his head through the wood of the door. "Yuck!" I heard him declare, from the other side. After a second's pause, he said, "It's a man's room... I think it's Starkey's... Yes, his name tag is on the suitcase... She's rifling through all of his stuff."

"What stuff?" I whispered. "Keep looking."

Grandad suddenly let out a moan. "Jay, she's coming back –
HIDE!"

I didn't have time to dash back to the end of the corridor, so I dived under a table, hoping she'd want to make a quick exit and wouldn't notice me. Just in time too, because the door creaked open and Chase peeked out.

Grandad staggered back, clutching his head. "Aargh! That did not feel good."

I clenched my eyes tight shut, waiting for her to pass. Next thing I knew a strong, determined hand gripped hold of my wrist and yanked me out from under the table.

I found myself on the floor, staring up into Chase Whitton's angry face.

"What are you doing?" she demanded.

My eyes shot to Grandad, but he'd be no help. He was leaning over, holding his head in his hands and moaning. The woman still gripped hold of my wrist, her hand like a vice. I decided it was time for my frightened kid routine. "I... I... I don't know, missus. I was just playing," I said, in a small, scared voice.

Her eyes softened. No one ever suspected a terrified kid. She leant closer and narrowed her eyes. "Tell no one you saw me here... Or else."

Chase flung my wrist at me, then strutted off back downstairs.

"Jayesh, son, are you OK?" Grandad rushed over. There was worry in his eyes; even he'd fallen for it.

"Oh, yes," I said, springing up and brushing myself down. "And now we know for sure."

"Know what?" Grandad asked.

We knew what no one else did, perhaps apart from Chase Whitton: "Starkey was murdered."

The Midnight Footsteps

I bumped into Mum and Granny coming up the stairs. Mum was dangling a doggie bag at her side.

"Food!" I cried.

"Mainly cheese," she replied, nibbling a piece of cheddar on a cracker. "The waiter said they had loads of it, they're just giving it away down there."

I glanced down the steps to the reception lobby, where sure enough a sweaty Parek was dishing out large portions of cheese from a trolley. "Take as much as you want," he was saying to the assembled guests. "Mr Shand made a mistake with his order at the dairy – we got too much this week."

Mr Shand, who was standing nearby, flushed. "You didn't have to tell them that, you fool!"

Back in our room, I gorged myself on cheese and crackers. A chicken burger it was not, but it was at least food.

"What now?" asked Grandad during a quiet moment when Granny was in the toilet and it was just the two of us.

With Mum and Granny around, I couldn't get away

with sneaking out of the room to snoop around. I'd at least have to wait until they were asleep. Which was incredibly annoying because as far as I was concerned, this was prime detecting time. There was lots of snooping to be done.

Perhaps I couldn't escape, but Grandad could. "You'll have to take a look around, Grandad."

His lip quivered. "What, in a strange old house, in the middle of the night?"

"You're a ghost, Grandad! You're the thing that normally scares people about old houses. You've nothing to be afraid of. You're also my top-secret weapon. So get out there, speak to the other ghosts if you can. See if they know anything."

"Pff!" Grandad said. "Some hope." He squeezed through the door. "Yuck! I HATE that!" Then he was gone.

Meanwhile, I dug out my notebook and got to work. First of all, I drew a map of the house:

ground floor

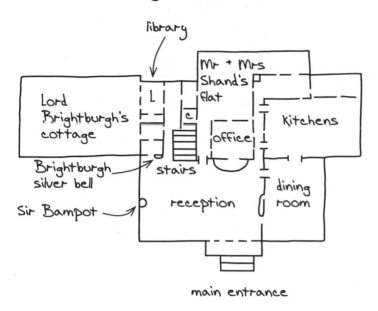

library

Mr + Mrs Shand's flat

Lord Brightburgh's cottage

Kitchens

office

Brightburgh silver bell

stairs

Sir Bampot

reception

dining room

main entrance

first floor

mum's room

my room

Starkey's room

65

Next, I drew up a list of suspects:

STAFF:
* Mr Shand: hotel owner, a bit miserable, scared of his wife!
* Mrs Shand: hotel owner, married to Mr Shand, VERY scary.
* Parek: waiter, sweats a lot, doesn't seem to like his job.
* Arek: porter, Parek's brother (or is it the other way around?), also sweats a lot, also doesn't seem to like his job.
* Chef: Swiss, bit of a lunatic, obsessed with something called 'fondue'.
* Lucy: goth receptionist, likes scowling – a lot!

GUESTS:
* Vera Hackenbottom: annoying old lady!
* Benedict Ravensbury: restaurant critic, history with the chef. Could that be a motive? Also a bit smug!
* Chase Whitton: Ravensbury's friend, definitely up to something – but what?
* Mum: slightly unhinged, but definitely not the murderer.
* Granny: completely unhinged, but definitely not the murderer.
* Me: obviously not the murderer!
* Grandad: deceased, so doesn't really count!

OTHERS
* Lord Brightburgh: ex-owner of house, went bankrupt and had to sell up (not too happy about it either!)

And then, on another page:

What is Chase Whitton up to?

As it stood, she had to be my prime suspect, so underneath I wrote:

PRIME SUSPECT

Thinking back to the dining room earlier, Chase mentioned that she used to be a nurse, before barging everyone out of the way to get to Starkey. Was that all a ruse to get close to him? Possibly. If his soup *was* poisoned then this gave her every chance of clearing away any evidence – didn't she wipe his face with a napkin?

Then again, if she was after something in his room, why bother to do the poor man in? Why, when she could just break into his room while he was at dinner and steal it for herself?

Before long all of these questions began to chase each other inside my head, and exhausted, I dozed off.

I dreamt about my Dad again.

I was back at home, and we were sitting around the dinner table, the whole family. Dad too. He was just as I remembered him: his eyes hazel brown, his hair jet black. He looked alive, as alive as he was before he disappeared.

Dad turned to me and opened his mouth to speak, but nothing came out. He was silent. I wondered why.

Grandad, on the other hand, was yelling at me. Loudly.

"Jayesh! Get up boy!"

I sat bolt upright in bed. It was the middle of the night.

"A fire?" I mumbled, stumbling out of bed, only to find Grandad stuck halfway through the door. He looked like one of the mounted stags heads downstairs in the reception, if they wore fedoras.

"Uh, these old wooden doors," he said. "They are a devil to get through. Did I mention I HATE walking through stuff?"

I couldn't say anything because I didn't want to wake Granny up. She's an extremely light sleeper, and it was a miracle that I hadn't woken her up already.

He tutted. "Hurry up, boy! There's something going on downstairs."

I creeped over and eased open the door, and he fell out with a loud *SCHLHHLOPP*, collapsing on the ground. "Uhh, I hate being a ghost," he groaned. As quietly as possible, I crept down the hall after Grandad. The corridor was pitch black and deathly silent. I imagined all the weird statues staring down at me, and the faces in the old paintings. It kind of gave me the creeps. It was dark down in the lobby too, the only faint light coming from lamps outside the windows.

I edged down the first few stairs. Grandad stopped, then turned and whispered, though I wasn't sure why as no one else could hear him except me. "There's someone creeping about down there. Look!"

I listened with bated breath. There was nothing for a few seconds, then the sound of furtive rustling, followed by a few light footsteps. The footsteps of someone trying to make as little noise as possible. Perhaps it was just one of the staff, but why would they be moving about in the dark? Surely they just would put a light on?

Grandad floated down to the foot of the steps. "Down here, Jayesh!"

I tiptoed down to the bottom to join him, then stopped.

The silence was broken by a loud **SMASH**. The crash of a heavy object connecting with glass. I nearly jumped out of my skin.

This was followed almost immediately by the ear-trembling shriek of an alarm going off nearby.

WEE-WAA-WEE-WAA!

"Owww!" I cupped my hands to my ears.

A black shape came at me out of the darkness. Someone's shoulder collided heavily with my own.

"OWWWW!" I tumbled to the ground.

"Jayesh!" Grandad shouted.

I lay there, dazed, before Grandad's greenish face loomed into mine. "Jayesh? You OK, boy?"

The footsteps raced away. I groaned and pulled myself to my feet, just as the lights were switched on.

Mr Shand and his wife were standing at an open door marked **PRIVATE**.

He was in his dressing gown and she had her curlers in, and her face looked ten times more frightening than any ghost.

They glared at me, shocked and horrified, then followed the trail of smashed glass from my feet to the display cabinet.

The plinth for the Brightburgh silver bell now stood empty.

"Uh-oh." I gulped.

Other guests were appearing at the top of the steps too, rubbing their eyes.

Shand's glare turned back in my direction, his face screwed up in anger.

"Uh-oh indeed," said Grandad.

CHAPTER 9

The Inside Job-eth?

DI Fallon had the look of a man who'd been forced out of his bed at one o'clock in the morning – tired, disheveled and bristling with hostility, mainly towards me.

A huge bear of a man, with a freckled face and a carpet of ginger hair, he squashed his large rear end into a bucket seat, his coat tails puffing up around the sides. "Right, tell me again, laddie," he growled.

"Look, there's nothing to tell," I said, holding up my hands. I sat facing him on one of the sofas in the lobby. "I heard noises downstairs, so I came down. Then I heard the crash. Someone barged into me, and I fell. When I got up, the lights came back on, and *he* was standing there."

I gestured at Shand, who sat beside the Inspector. He jabbed an accusing finger at me. "You were asking about the silver bell earlier, when you arrived. You even talked about stealing it."

"He has got a point," Grandad called over from behind the reception desk, where I'd sent him to snoop around.

"Oh, please belt up!" I snapped, forgetting myself.

Shand bridled. "D-Don't you tell me to belt up, young man!"

Mrs Shand was behind the couch, clutching her dressing gown. She leant in and now she too jabbed a finger in my direction. "See, I told you! Riff-raff." She sniffed. "I did say no riff-raff, Timothy."

Mum was sitting beside me, her arm wrapped round my shoulder. The alarm hadn't woken her. To be fair, no alarm in the world could wake Mum up. She went to sleep listening to whale noises, which were a million times more annoying. They had to physically barge into her room and shake her awake.

Now she leapt to her feet and fixed Mrs Shand with

a terrifying glare. The good-natured, earth-loving people-person evaporated. She snorted, flared her nostrils and flexed her fists. She was like a prize fighter squaring up for a fight. "Who are you callin' riff-raff, ya boot?" she snarled in broad Glaswegian.

Granny had been standing beside the sofa too, her arms folded, watching everything through narrowed eyes. She leapt in the air like a mountain cougar pouncing upon its prey and landed right in front of Mrs Shand, one hand steadying herself against the floor and the other balancing in the air. She looked up from under her eyebrows and growled. "You're gettin' it, blancmange heid!"

Mrs Shand touched a quivering hand to her hair, then scurried back through the door marked PRIVATE. Even Fallon looked a tiny bit terrified, and he was a copper.

A mushy grin came across Grandad's face and he clapped his ghostly hands in front of his chest. "Ah, what a tiger she is, that granny of yours."

"Look," I said to the Inspector. "If I'd nicked the silver bell then where is it? I don't have it. I mean, what am I supposed to have done with it? Hidden it in my pyjamas?"

Fallon scrutinised me from under his huge ginger eyebrows, then he turned to Shand. "How long was it between the alarm going off and you switching the lights on?"

"Not long, a few seconds. Our bedroom is just through the back there."

"Hmm." Fallon rubbed his stubbly chin with his giant hand. He flipped open his notebook and scored something out, then he sighed loudly, as if my lack of guilt was an inconvenience. "The laddie is right."

"What?" Shand was disappointed.

Fallon grunted, then prised himself out of the chair. "It might have been one of the local hoodies. I'll round them up and we'll see whit's whit."

"Hoodies?" I asked, confused.

"Aye, laddie. Hoodies. Gangs of boys that hang around street corners wearing hooded tops. I don't like hoodies much." Fallon evidently hadn't finished, as this soon turned into a rant. "I mean, what kind of fashion statement does that make? I'll tell you what kind of statement that makes. It says, 'I'm up to no good'."

Grandad floated out from behind the reception desk. "Huh! A man was poisoned and he's going on about jumpers! Tell him, Jayesh! Tell him a man was poisoned."

I glanced over at Grandad and shook my head. Fallon didn't know that. Not yet. He was here to investigate the silver bell being stolen. As far as he, or anyone else was concerned, there was nothing suspicious about a man dropping dead in his soup over dinner. They might pick the poison up in a few days in a post-mortem. Then again, they might not. I could have told them about Starkey, but that would just throw more suspicion on me.

Grandad suddenly spotted something near the display case. "Jayesh, come over here!" He pointed at the floor. "There's a feather. Here on the floor. Could that be important?"

It might be, so while Fallon and Shand were talking, I strolled over, knelt down and had a look. It was a feather, sure enough. Tiny and white, the kind you get inside a... "Pillow," I said.

"What?" growled Fallon.

"I think there might be something over here, a feather. It's from a pillow. Whoever smashed the cabinet tried to muffle the sound, but it didn't really work."

Fallon fixed me with a steely, assessing stare then nodded, turning to Shand. "Where would they get a pillow from?"

The manager shrugged. "There's a laundry cart down the corridor there, but it's kept in a store cupboard when it isn't in use."

Shand led Fallon down the corridor to show him the cupboard, while Grandad danced behind the reception desk to show me something else. "One of the drawers in here has been broken open with a crowbar. I bet you it is where they keep the cash. Do not tell them, mind you, because they have not noticed it yet. It will just give them another reason to think it was you."

"A-ha!" I whispered, leaning out of earshot of Mum and Granny. "So, whoever the burglar was, they knew where the cash was kept, and they knew where the laundry cart was too. You know what that means, don't you?"

Grandad scratched his head. "Uh... it was a thief with an interest in housekeeping?"

"No, it was an inside job. Either one of the staff, or one of the guests."

"A-ha! Exact-amundo!" said Grandad. "An inside job."

"What's that, dearie?" Mum called over.

"Oh, nothing," I replied.

Fallon and Shand returned from the corridor, while a uniformed officer entered from the kitchen. The officer touched Fallon's arm and whispered in his ear.

Fallon nodded, and turned to us. "We found a broken window pane on the kitchen door. It seems that's how the burglar gained entry." He led Shand through the back.

"Oooh, how exciting," said Mum. "I want to see this,

I'm going with them." She trailed after the two men.

"Me n'all," croaked Granny, rolling up her sleeves and following close behind, leaving me and Grandad alone.

"While they're gone," I eyed the suit of armour nearby, "why don't you ask that ghost if he saw anything?"

"What, Sir Bampot? No thanks." Grandad shook his head.

"Oh, go on," I whined. "It's important!"

Grandad sighed, then blinked his eyes. "There. You ask him!"

I found myself staring at the grotesque face poking out of the helmet visor, one jelly-like eyeball swinging loose.

"Fine," I said. Up close, I could see the skull had tiny phantom maggots crawling out of it. "Excuse me, sir. I don't suppose you saw who stole the silver bell?"

"I saweth naught!" the spectre growled. "It was too darketh!"

"Are you sureth?" Oops. Adding '–eth' to the end of everything seemed to be catching.

"Are you mocking how I speaketh?!" he hissed. "How dareth you challenge me! Cometh here whilst I smite you."

"See! He's at the smiting again!" Grandad backed away. "You'll get no sense out of that one."

"Do you know what," I said, throwing up my hands, "Grandad, you're right. This is useless. This witness is useless."

"Useless-eth," corrected Grandad. He blinked, and the other ghost was gone.

"Hmmm..." I propped myself against the back of one

of the armchairs. My mind was whirring like clockwork. I imagined pieces of a jigsaw emerging from a mist and shifting around, trying to find their place: the Yummy Cola letter, Sharkey's poisoning, that Chase woman poking around in Starkey's room. And now this, a priceless silver bell, stolen. All of it must be connected, but how? Surely it couldn't be a coincidence that all of this had happened on the very day we'd arrived? Try as I might, nothing fitted together. Not yet.

"OK," said Grandad attempting to lean against a sofa, but failing. "The Yummy Cola letter was probably fake. Which means someone wanted you here, but why?"

"Oh, so now you agree, the letter's fake?"

Before Grandad had the chance to reply, I felt the armchair behind me move. It seemed we weren't alone.

You're a strange boy, aren't you?" It was Mrs Hackenbottom, sitting with her feet up, wearing a pink fluffy dressing gown and matching slippers, and reading an Agatha Christie book. I had no idea she was there, and neither did Grandad, because he jumped. When the alarm had gone off earlier, lots of the guests had appeared, milling about in the lobby for a bit before the alarm was shut off again and the excitement died down, when most of them returned to bed. Mrs Hackenbottom must have been sitting there the whole time, listening, snooping. I had to hand it to her for her detective skills. If even I didn't notice her, that was some top-level sneaking.

"Talking to yourself?" she continued.

"Och! Not that old bag!" cried Grandad.

Mrs Hackenbottom hauled herself noisily to her feet, and waved her book around. "I'm quite the amateur detective too, you know. Why don't we investigate this matter together?"

"Erm, I..." The old crone had caught me off guard.

She hobbled round the armchair and linked her arm in mine. "So it's a deal, we'll solve this case together."

"No way!" Grandad shook his head. "I am not investigating anything with that woman. She's too nosy for her own good, and she spits food when she eats!"

"It'll be fun," Mrs Hackenbottom cackled, crinkling her mouth into a satisfied grin.

CHAPTER 10

The Reeky Ruins

Morning finally arrived, and I rolled out of bed and rubbed my eyes. The sun was streaming through the gaps in the curtains, and Grandad was reclined on an armchair, floating, his hands clasped behind his head.

"Thought you'd never wake up!" he quipped.

I glanced quickly over at Granny's bamboo roll mat. It was empty. She'd probably been up for ages. She usually woke at dawn for karate training.

"Did you manage to find anything?" I'd asked Grandad to keep an eye on things overnight, and try and speak to some of the ghosts. He hadn't been very happy about that.

"Not really," he said. "The place is stinking with ghosts, but most of them are just phantoms." From what I could understand, there weren't many ghosts like Grandad, who you could have a conversation with, and who behaved pretty much like they did when they were alive. Most of them were just imprints, reflections of people reliving moments from time gone by – phantoms, as Grandad called them. You couldn't communicate with them, and they didn't communicate with you.

"There is one guy wandering around the first floor with a cigar and wearing a smoking jacket, who looks like he might have been shot. And there is another man, a tall man, who haunts the kitchen carrying a pail. I think he took kicking the bucket literally. There are a few more, but they are all like our friend in the suit of armour."

"You got nothing out of them? Nothing at all?"

He shrugged. "There is a strange Grey Lady. Horrible she is. She stands outside, in front of the window, her face pressed up against the glass, staring in. She seems to want me to follow her somewhere."

"You should have gone with her," I said.

"Are you kidding? Follow a strange ghost? Not on your nelly."

"How about Starkey's ghost? Isn't he still here?"

Grandad shook his head.

There was a knock at the connecting door. "Jay?" It was Mum. "You coming for breakfast?"

"I'll see you down there," I shouted, and started pulling on my clothes and trainers. Then I flicked through the pages of my notebook. "We need to know more about Starkey. Someone wanted him dead. We need to know why."

"Dead men don't talk," Grandad declared wisely. "Maybe he knew something... about something."

"Useful. But no, I'm pretty sure it's all linked to the hotel," I said. "There's the burglary, then the fact that Shand is bankrupt and trying to sell the hotel. We should think about motive. Who's got the motive to poison guests, and who's got the motive to steal the silver bell?"

Grandad clapped his hands together. "How about that Lord Brightburgh guy?"

"That's exactly what I was thinking." I threw open the curtain to see Granny in the middle of the wide lawn, furiously going through her karate moves while a peacock strutted around her, spreading its feathers. "He said it was disgraceful, what they've done to this place. Maybe he wants them to go out of business so that he can take back his old ancestral pile."

"Ooh, he could have staged the break in," suggested Grandad. "You cannot get more of an inside job than the old Lord of the Manor who lives next door."

"I bet he'd love to get that silver bell back – for sentimental reasons. It must be very hard seeing someone else walk off with the family silver and then flaunt it in your face. Except, he was away last night. Edinburgh, he said. If that's true then he might have an alibi."

"Hmm..." Grandad stroked his chin like the detectives on the TV shows he liked to watch. "So how could Lord Brightburgh have stolen the bell if he wasn't around?"

Downstairs in the lobby, the glass from the shattered display cabinet had been cleaned up, and there was no sign of any police. There was a chill in the air, as if someone had left a back door open somewhere. Shand was sitting at a desk behind reception, while the receptionist, Lucy was stomping around slamming drawers and fuming.

"You can't talk to me like that!" she growled through clenched teeth.

"I only asked you to pass the stapler," replied Shand.

"Oh, well, one day," she seethed, jabbing her finger at him, "things are going to change. Maybe I'll be the one ordering *you* about."

She landed the stapler with a dunt in front of Shand, and then stomped off out the back.

Shand threw out his arms in protest. **"What?!"**

Grandad shooed me away from the reception desk towards the front door. "I want to show you something."

Outside, the sky was blue but the air was chilly, and a lone crow cawed in the trees. "Up there." Grandad pointed up at some old ruins clustered round a hillock a few hundred yards away. The glistening waters of Loch Lomond, and its forested islands, stretched out behind. "That's where she wants me to go."

"Who?"

"The Grey Lady, the one I told you about."

"Oh." Apart from the view up the loch, the ruins themselves looked bleak and uninteresting. Arek, the porter was nearby, leaning over the boot of a hatchback loading up suitcases.

"I'll ask," I said, and walked up to Arek. "Excuse me."

"Yes?" Arek looked up, breathing heavily.

"See those ruins?" I pointed up at them. "Any idea what they are?"

"That is just the old tower." His face darkened. "I would not go up there if I were you."

"Why not?"

He sniffed. "It is not safe." He pointed his finger at a red danger sign hanging on the fence. Then he heaved another suitcase into the boot.

"Did something happen up there?"

He wiped his brow with his sleeve, and spoke quietly. "The lady died up there a few years ago. They said it was a freak accident. Part of the ruins collapsed. They say it is safe now, but I for one would not go up there." He shivered.

"That boy is a wee bit psychic, if you ask me," said Grandad. "He can tell it is haunted. Ask him who she was, the woman."

"*The* lady, you say?" As in, not *a* lady.

The porter leant even closer, his voice but a whisper. "It was Lord Brightburgh's wife. The Lady Brightburgh. I am surprised you did not hear about it. It was in the newspapers. She managed the whole estate. Without her it all went kaputt. It was not long afterwards that Lord Brightburgh went bankrupt and had to sell it all. He lost everything, the poor man. They never had any children, so he is the very last in his line."

A bell ding in reception made the porter's ears prick up. "Oh, I have to go." He rushed inside in a panic.

"Hmm..." I stared at the ruins. "I wonder."

"Lady Brightburgh could be the Grey Lady," said Grandad. "All I know is, she is fairly keen on showing me something. It could be important. It might have something to do with what's going on."

"We'll go up there later," I agreed. But for now I was hungry and needed to eat.

"Are you sure you want to eat anything from this place?" Grandad asked as he followed me inside. "It might be poisoned."

I was so hungry I didn't even think that would stop me. It was easy to poison soup. A murderer could easily dissolve a substance into liquid. It wasn't so easy to poison a bacon roll, of which I was planning to eat many. Anyhow, Starkey wasn't the only person to have the soup, but he was the only one poisoned, which meant that he was targeted specifically. As we passed the reception, I noticed Mr Shand sitting miserably behind the desk being berated by Mrs Shand.

Funnily enough I'd just been thinking about Shand. The hotel was obviously in trouble, maybe even close to being shut down. Was it possible that he *wanted* it to close? As for the silver bell, was it possible he faked the break in and stole it himself, hoping for a big insurance payout?

In the dining room, Mum had found a table. Unfortunately, she wasn't alone.

CHAPTER 11

The Big Cheese

"Oh, great!" Grandad tutted. "Is there no escaping that old bat!"

Mrs Hackenbottom sat with Mum at our table, looking as nosy as ever.

"Morning," I mumbled, sitting down. I knocked my knee against the table leg, which sent a butter knife clattering off the plate and over the edge. Mrs Hackenbottom jerked her wrist and snatched it before it hit the ground.

"Good morning," she said, flipping the knife round, then using it to scoop up a huge pat of butter and smear it on a piece of toast. The fact that she and a number of other diners were stuffing their faces without frothing at the mouth was an encouraging sign. "You know," she bit off a chunk and waved the rest of the toast at me, "your mother is a lovely woman, but she's quite distant."

I glanced at Mum. Her eyes were closed, and her face was stuck with that vacant grin of hers.

Mrs Hackenbottom continued. "She hasn't spoken to me once. I was beginning to think she'd been poisoned too."

The mere mention of the p-word was enough to turn a few nervous heads in the room. The horrible grating sound of her voice probably didn't help.

"Don't worry," I said. "She does this every morning. She's earth-healing."

"I beg your pardon?"

"Aye!" Grandad chipped in. "I sometimes cannot believe my son married this fruitcake." I glared at Grandad, who held up his hands. "I love her to bits though."

I turned back to Mrs Hackenbottom. "It's a kind of meditating. You picture the world, and then you imagine it slowly healing itself."

For once, Mrs Hackenbottom didn't quite know what to say.

I took my chance to flag down the waiter, Parek. "Excuse me!"

Parek seemed flustered, just as flustered as his twin brother had been about five minutes earlier. "Sorry," he panted, "we're short-staffed. We're *always* short-staffed."

"Listen carefully," I said. "I'll have seven bacon rolls, please."

"Is that all?" he asked, in a sarcastic tone.

"You're right. I'll take eight just to be sure."

Grandad chortled. "That is one hungry boy."

I rubbed my hands and tucked in my napkin. "I'm going to enjoy this."

Mrs Hackenbottom stared at me for a moment, chewing on her toast. "I've been thinking," she said. "We should investigate the other guests." She nodded at a couple sitting at the table in the corner. Quiet, middle-aged, they looked harmless. "That's Mr and Mrs Bullard from Basingstoke." Then she turned and motioned towards a woman sitting on her own reading a birdwatching book, a pair of binoculars propped up beside her on the table. "That lady is called Mrs Neasden, and she's from Devon. Up here to gaze at herons or something. There's also a couple from Fife, but they're leaving."

Apart from that, not many other guests remained, except Benedict Ravensbury and Chase Whitton, who weren't at their table, and the party of German golfers on holiday.

Grandad scoffed. "I am not staying here listening to her. I am going to sit with someone else."

He wandered over to Mrs Neasden's table and plonked himself down on an empty chair next to her. "Hello!"

Mrs Neasden didn't respond, of course. She was halfway through her kippers.

Ravensbury entered, fidgeting with his cuffs. He combed back a lock of hair from his forehead, then flagged down Parek. "Excuse me, have you seen my friend, Ms Whitton? She isn't in her room."

I eyed their table. The place settings hadn't been touched. The waiter shrugged and rushed off to the kitchen, while Ravensbury glanced about nervously and then left the dining room.

I glanced meaningfully over at Grandad.

"I bet she's snooping around somewhere," he said.

"I bet she is," I muttered back. And I intended to find out why. I whipped off my napkin and stood up.

"What's that?" said Mrs Hackenbottom. "Where are you off to?"

"HEEAALL THE WORRRLLLLD!" Mum wailed through her vacant grin.

"The bathroom," I lied, and nodded Grandad towards the door.

Outside in the lobby, I watched Ravensbury traipse up the steps towards the bedrooms. I paused there for a second, feeling the prickles on my skin again – there was a definite draught out here, and it was coming from somewhere behind the stairs.

"What is it, son?" asked Grandad, reading my expression.

Following my instincts, I slipped down the corridor behind the staircase. There were no bedrooms down here, just a series of doors marked PRIVATE. One of the doors was slightly ajar. I raised my hand towards the crack, feeling cold air seep out from inside. This was definitely where the draught was coming from.

I creaked the door open. It was pitch black inside, and dusty smelling. A set of worn stone steps led downwards into blackness.

Grandad shivered. "I hate cellars. They are spooky." Which was a bit rich given that he was the spook.

I yanked a cord that was hanging down and a light came on, a bare bulb suspended from the ceiling.

The walls were stark and cold. "After you," said Grandad, hanging back.

"Some ghost you are," I muttered, and gingerly stepped down towards the foot of the stairs.

At the bottom, it looked as if a set of shelves had toppled over, as there was a pile of debris on the floor: splinters of broken wood and a huge, round, buff-coloured object. I spotted something lying underneath, a shape. And then, with a growing sense of dread, I realised it wasn't some*thing* but some*one*.

I then saw a slender wrist hanging limply, an ankle sticking out, and finally some tendrils of curly dark hair and emerald green fabric.

It was Chase Whitton, her face and upper body hidden underneath the large object on top of her. What *was* that? It was too round for a cardboard box, and its surface was smoother. Whatever it was, it was large and extremely heavy. It had crushed the poor woman underneath.

"Cheese wheel," said Grandad. "I used to sell them to restaurants from my cash and carry."

"Cheese what?" I asked.

"A massive wheel of cheese," he clarified.

I leant down and pressed my thumb against her wrist. There was no pulse, and her skin was as cold as stone.

"She's dead," I said.

"I can see that," replied Grandad.

I gazed up to see him staring into space just above the body. He was watching something.

"What is it?" I asked.

He turned his gaze on me and then blinked. Now I could see it too.

Or rather her, Chase Whitton. Well, her ghost, anyway. She couldn't see us, and all we saw was an imprint of her last moments.

She whisked around, facing the direction the shelves had toppled from. Her eyes widened with shock and fear. "You!" she cried. Then she held her arms up, apparently to protect her face. "No, NOOOO!" She disappeared, only to reappear a second later and repeat the whole scene again.

"She is nothing but a phantom; like a recording, played over and over," said Grandad.

I gazed down at the wreckage on the floor. Someone had deliberately pushed over the shelves and crushed her to death with a massive wheel of cheese. What was it about this place and food? I was just starting to think about who that someone could be when there came a horrible high-pitched scream behind me.

I whirled round to see Mrs Shand at the top of the stairs. She was trembling so much her beehive was quaking, with bits of hair falling out of place. One hand covered her mouth, the other she raised in the air and pointed, direct and accusing, straight at me, as she cried out:

"MURDERER!"

The Terrible Twins

The grandfather clock chimed a quarter to the hour. The Brightburgh Manor library was at the back of the house, looking out onto the gardens, with rows of walnut cabinets lined with old books. DI Fallon glared down at me from beneath his bushy eyebrows. He was sitting high up behind an antique desk. I, meanwhile, was squashed into the tiniest chair imaginable. It looked like a chair for a toddler. I could have sworn he'd chosen it deliberately to make me look ridiculous.

I held up my hands. "I'm the first to admit, it doesn't look good."

"No, laddie, it doesn't," he replied.

"Maybe you should just tell him everything," said Grandad, who was floating around near the window.

But why should I do that? I was already under enough suspicion. It would just make me look like the chief suspect. Fallon was lazy, I could tell. Lazy enough to pin the murders on me? I didn't want to test him.

"Look, she was cold when I found her," I said to Fallon. "She'd been dead for a while, a few hours maybe." By my reckoning, it must have happened some time after the police left and everyone went to bed, and before the hotel began to wake up.

"Aye," he said. "That's true. But you could have murdered her, then returned to the crime scene later to pretend you found her."

"He has got a point," chirped Grandad. I glowered at him. Wasn't he supposed to be on my side?

"I'm sharing a room with my granny," I insisted. "I couldn't have left without her noticing." Which wasn't actually true, I'd already done it. But coming from the mouth of an eleven year old it sounded believable.

"Oh no?" One of Fallon's bushy ginger eyebrows rose. "By the way, we are now treating the death of the man at dinner last night as suspicious too."

About time, I thought. They should've been treating it as suspicious from the off. The only problem – and it was a pretty humungous one – was that all that suspicion seemed to be pointing in my direction.

"Look, that was nothing to do with me, apart from the fact I was sitting at the next table," I said.

"Exactly!" he declared. "You were sitting right next to him, perfectly positioned. You know, if you are innocent, then you have a knack of showing up at exactly the wrong place at exactly the wrong time. And let me tell you," he leant forward, "I don't like that. I don't like that at all."

"Tch! Charming!" said Grandad.

Fallon crooked his head, inspecting my neck. "Here, you don't wear hooded tops, do you?"

The truth was that sometimes I did, but I got the feeling that being honest wouldn't do me any favours, so I lied. "No, never. Wouldn't be seen dead in one."

"Good. Cos let me tell you something, as soon as you start wearing hooded tops it's a slippery slope. One moment you're in a shop buying a hoodie, next thing you know, you're skipping school, loitering in public places, kicking in windows..."

"What is it with this guy and hooded tops?" asked Grandad.

"And then," Fallon continued, "you're just a short step away from robbing old ladies, and car-jackings, and bank heists, and the very worst crimes imaginable."

Grandad puffed out his cheeks. "This guy is absolutely nuts."

Fallon leaned back and tapped his pen on the desk. "But, I've got nothing solid on you. Not yet anyway. You can go, for now. But remember..." He jabbed two fingers towards his own eyes, then turned them round and jabbed them at me. "I'm watching you, laddie!"

And he wasn't wrong. He watched me intensely, glared at me in fact, as I tried, and failed, to dislodge myself from the tiny chair. He kept watching as I gave up and waddled, half-bent, out of the door with the daft toddler chair still lodged on my rear end.

"Well, he cannot complain, you were glued to your seat throughout," quipped Grandad.

"Oh, hilarious." I shot him a look. It took me about five minutes to prise myself out of the thing. Grandad just laughed the whole time.

In reception, forensic officers wearing white head-to-toe uniforms were scuttling between the front door, the cellar and the dining room. I joined Mum and Granny, who were both standing around and looking on along with everyone else. I scanned the faces. Anxious guests and staff hanging about in small groups, mumbling their worries to each other.

Meanwhile, Mr Bullard and his wife were in Shand's face, shouting, "We're leaving! We're leaving this instant!" Their bags were piled at their feet.

Shand's jacket was off, hanging on the back of a chair nearby. He'd rolled up his shirtsleeves and there were patches of sweat under his arms. He was shuffling nervously, waving them down with his hands. "Please! Please!"

"No, we won't stay here a moment longer!" Bullard barked. "People dropping like flies, the food clearly poisoned, burglaries in the middle of the night! Why on earth would we want to stay?"

"Maybe we should go too?" I said to Mum. No one would blame me for walking away from this, I thought, except perhaps whoever sent the fake Yummy Cola letter. They wanted me here for a reason, I just didn't know what it was yet.

"Whit!" croaked Granny, rolling up her sleeves. "This is just gettin' interesting!"

"Oh no, I wouldn't dream of leaving," replied Mum. "These people need my healing energies around the place."

The party of German golfers were the only ones who looked like they were having a good time. Judging by the notepads and pens they were scribbling on, they seemed to think they were part of some kind of murder mystery weekend. They were comparing notes and arguing over who they thought the murderer was. Worryingly, three of them were pointing their pens at me. Boy, I thought, I'm going to have to solve this case, and solve it fast!

"Please!" shouted Shand, coming out from behind the desk and raising his voice so that everyone could hear. "I'm... I'm afraid that the police have told us no one is allowed to leave. You're free to go about the hotel, and the village, but no further."

There was an audible gasp, followed by a hubbub as the crowd all gathered round to gossip.

The chef appeared. This time he was armed with a garlic press. He prowled around the lobby, waving his finger at people randomly. "There's nothing wrong with my food! Understand?" he kept saying.

"If I could just taste some," I said, "I might be able to confirm that. Perhaps a boiled egg or a sausage?" By this point, I was so hungry that no amount of poison in the world would stop me eating something.

The chef glared at me, his eye twitching. Granny glared back at him, and his garlic press, then bowed respectfully, as if he was a great opponent. I clearly wasn't going to get that sausage any time soon.

Parek the waiter came bounding into the hall, panting and wiping sweat from his brow. Shand beckoned him over. "Parek, come here!"

I took the chance to do a bit more digging and tapped Shand on the shoulder. "Excuse me, but do you perhaps have any enemies at all? Anyone who might want to cause you, or the hotel, some trouble?"

He glared at me, insulted. "How dare you! Of course I don't. I'm actually very well liked, ask anyone."

"Ha!" Parek shot him a look, one that I could only describe as murderous.

"Could you please find your brother, Arek," said Shand to the waiter, tersely. "Mr Bullard's bags need to go back up to his room."

The waiter scowled and gave Shand one final death-like stare before turning and sprinting through the back, loosening his tie as he went.

I whispered at Grandad, "Did you see that look the waiter gave Shand?"

"I think we should check him out, and his brother as well. Twins are suspicious."

"Yes," I agreed. "Quick!" I made to follow the waiter down the corridor behind the kitchens.

"Hey!" said Grandad, halting to crane his neck back towards reception. "Look at Mrs Hackenbottom. What's the old bat doing now?"

I stepped back and carefully poked my head around the wall to see the old lady crawling on all fours behind the reception desk. She didn't think anyone else could see her, but she didn't reckon on me. She reached her arm up towards Shand's jacket, which was hanging over the chair.

I ducked out of sight. "She's muscling in on our investigation," I said. She was after Shand, which was understandable. I wanted to check him out more myself, but right now we were following a hot trail of our own. "Later. Come on!" I continued down the corridor after Parek.

At the end, I caught a glimpse of the waiter as he pushed his way through a narrow white door that looked like the entrance to a store cupboard. Why would he go in there?

I paused outside the door and listened – nothing. I knocked – still nothing. Then I quietly pushed it open.

Inside was an empty store cupboard. Brooms were stacked on one side. There was a manky old sink and a mirror. And there was no sign of Parek.

"Where did he go?" asked Grandad, which was exactly what I was thinking.

Then I saw that there was another door inside, an even narrower one. I pulled it open. A set of very narrow, very old stone steps led upwards. "Wow!" I knew this place had to be full of stuff like this. "A secret passageway!"

"Come on then!" said Grandad, and I led the way up.

The stairs wound endlessly upwards. I guessed that in

the old days these must have been the servants' stairs or something. Eventually we came to another door, which opened onto a silent corridor.

Grandad floated out behind me. "Where are we?"

"Top floor," I whispered. I could tell because of the dormer windows looking out onto the grounds. "Also the staff quarters."

"How do you know that?"

I pointed out the décor, the walls and the carpet, which were a lot less plush than the rest of the hotel. The wallpaper was faded and the carpet looked like a relic from the 1970s.

"Ooh, nice carpet," said Grandad, which proved my point.

I sneaked down the corridor and peeked around a corner to see Parek halting at a door right at the far end.

"That must be his room," guessed Grandad. He floated ahead. "I will sneak in behind him."

As the waiter opened the door, Grandad gave me the thumbs up, then snuck in at his back. The door slammed shut. I crept along the corridor and stuck my ear against it, listening.

It was only a few seconds before Grandad's voice called from the other side. "Jayesh! You can come in, it is unlocked. But be quiet!"

I grasped the handle and twisted gently. The door edged open and Grandad's face peered out. "Quick!" He beckoned me inside.

It was a large room with two twin beds: one, I assumed, for each of the brothers. Parek's clothes were scattered over one of them. The bathroom door was shut and I could hear taps running on the other side.

"He is definitely our chief suspect," nodded Grandad. "You know what he just said there when he was getting undressed? He kept saying 'I hate him! I hate him!' under his breath, then he said, 'I know what I'd like to do to you, Shand!' And he grabbed a towel, like this." Grandad made a violent twisting motion with his hands.

"Maybe Shand's just a really bad boss," I whispered.

"You know what else?" said Grandad, but before he could go on the sound of the running taps suddenly stopped. Grandad made a shoo-ing motion and I jumped behind an armchair, just as the bathroom door opened.

The waiter was muttering to himself as he came out, "Always giving orders... Fetch this! Carry this! Lift that!" He growled with anger. "Oh, I HATE him so much!"

"YESSS!" Grandad shouted. "I knew it!"

I sensed Parek turning towards the window, where he had his back to me, so I peeked over the top of the armchair. Except there was no waiter there.

It was the porter, Arek – Parek's brother.

"Wait!" Grandad nipped into the bathroom, craned his head round, and nipped back out again. "That is what I was going to tell you. The waiter went in there carrying the porter's uniform. And, wait for it, there is no one else in the bathroom."

Arek turned back, fixing his collar, and I ducked. His footsteps crossed the room, and he flung open the door and walked out.

"Which means..." Grandad continued.

I stepped out from behind the armchair. "The waiter and the porter are the same man!"

CHAPTER 13

The Deadly Gargoyle

"Oh come on, boy," tutted Grandad as I vaulted the driveway fence, ignoring the red **⚠ DANGER** sign, and marched across the grass. We were heading towards the ruins. Grandad of course didn't need to jump the fence, he just floated through it. "You have got to admit, on a scale of 1–10 for suspicious, that Arek – or Parek – is a 9 at least."

"I'm not so sure about that," I said. "Plenty of people don't like their bosses. Anyway, there's no evidence linking him." We'd rummaged through his drawers, finding payslips for both Arek and Parek, but little else.

"He is a crook!!" said Grandad.

"Yeah, he's obviously a fraud. One guy claiming two salaries. But apart from that, I'm not sure he's a murderer – or a thief. We just need more evidence." Evidence that I was in a hurry to obtain, before suspicion came any closer to landing on me.

"At least we know now why he sweats so much," Grandad laughed.

We came to the ruins, mostly just a pile of old stones

covered in moss and lichen. Tendrils of mist were feeling their way across the deserted remains.

"Look." I kicked over a broken stone carving, which looked like a kind of grinning imp, resting its head in its hands and sticking out its tongue. Grandad shrugged. We took a few more steps through the mist, then he flung his arm across my chest, forgetting that I would just walk through it. "There she is again." Grandad was staring at a fixed point a few metres away, next to the wall.

"What does she look like?" I asked.

"I'll show you." He blinked.

Suddenly, I could see her. A faint grey figure of a middle-aged woman, she looked to be wearing a wax jacket and wellies, and carrying a dog lead in her hand.

"Can she see us? Can we talk to her?"

"No, she is a phantom, like Chase Whitton's ghost. And she is very faint. Almost faded away completely."

From what Grandad told me, most phantoms are like footprints in the sand, they slowly get washed away by time.

The woman jerked her head up, staring at a spot where a wall might once have stood. "No!" she cried. "Not... GARGOYLE!" She threw her hands up to protect her face and screamed.

Grandad glanced again at the grinning stone imp and whistled. "Death by gargoyle, that's a new one."

"Did someone murder you?" I asked the ghost. "Who was it?" But the ghost didn't respond. I turned to Grandad, thinking he'd be more useful, being a ghost himself. "Ask her who! Ask her who!"

"I am trying! I am trying! But she is hardly there at all. She is just like a recording, playing over and over again to anybody who will listen."

"S... S... Sunshine girl!" declared the ghost, floating slowly towards us. "The sunshine girl!"

"The sunshine girl, eh? Well, that could be a clue," said Grandad.

"Yes, but for what? Who knows what she's talking about?" I answered.

"I must tell them, I must warn them," repeated the woman, and she passed through us, heading towards the house.

"There she goes." Grandad watched her with sad eyes. "Off to the house to stare in through the windows, trying to warn people of the danger. She'll be back here in a second, just wait."

Sure enough, the phantom returned across the grounds, wailing, "Danger, danger!" Then she passed above the ruins and hovered over the crest of the hill, silhouetted against the blue waters of the loch, where she pointed down at something.

Grandad floated over to the edge of the steep slope on the other side of the ruins. "She is pointing down there."

I joined him, staring down towards the bushes and trees at the bottom.

"Down." Grandad made a downward motion with his hands. "We need to go down and see."

"Come on, then." I started edging down the slope.

"Ugh! I hate being a ghost," said Grandad, following behind me.

"It's alright for you, you can just float," I replied. "I have to climb all the way down, then climb back up again."

At the bottom, Grandad stopped and looked around. We

were both waiting for the Grey Lady to show us, or at least be slightly more specific as to what we should be looking for, but she didn't. Instead, she just turned and floated back up the hill, before disappearing altogether.

"Why here?" I asked. There was nothing except rocks and mud and a few sheep droppings.

"I do not know." Grandad shrugged. "And I do not think you will get anything else from her. She is just a poor lost spirit. She gets squashed by a gargoyle. Then she goes to the house and she searches for someone to tell, to warn. She comes back up to the ruins, and then she goes down here." We stood for a moment, listening to the sounds of cows mooing somewhere on the distant banks of the loch. Grandad pulled out his sunglasses and put them on. "I hate the countryside."

I kicked around for a few moments, nosing into the bushes. You never know what you might find. Maybe she was trying to lead us to an important clue. "I wonder," I said. "If that ghost really is Lady Brightburgh, and she really was killed by a gargoyle, then is her death all those years ago linked to what's going on here today?"

"I would not bet against it, son," said Grandad. "I would not bet against it at all."

The Terrible Tandem

Grandad halted abruptly as we were halfway back across the field. "Look."

He nodded towards the tail end of a car that was parked round the side of the manor house, a green Triumph Spitfire. The other half of the car was obscured by a line of trees. "That car was not there when we left."

The licence plate read:

"LB 1 – Lord Brightburgh. He must've come back."

I could see two figures moving about through the trees. "Come on, let's snoop." I ran to my left, ducking behind a hedge that ran parallel to the house. Grandad wasn't ducking, he had no need to. "What do you see?" I asked.

"It's him, alright. He's talking to that receptionist."

"Lucy." The goth.

"They're facing the other way, so you can probably sneak a quick look, but be careful."

I peeked over the top of the hedge to find we were overlooking a cottage garden. A line of tall sunflowers led up to the bright yellow door of a cottage. The cottage was attached to the main house. I assumed this was where Lord Brightburgh lived.

The two of them were standing close together next to an open gate marked PRIVATE. Closer, I thought, than you'd expect two apparently unrelated people to stand. Friendly close, like they were sharing a secret. He lifted a small overnight bag from the car's boot. There was something nagging at me, something at the back of my mind, something I was struggling to work out.

Just then, Lucy turned in my direction. I ducked, fast enough, I hoped, that she wouldn't have spotted me.

Grandad sucked sharply through his teeth.

"Did she see?" I whispered.

"She saw something, cos she looked right at us, but I do not think she saw you. It is OK though, she turned away and kept talking."

A moment later, the pair separated. Lord Brightburgh went inside the cottage while Lucy turned and stomped off, up the drive and away from the house. "Maybe she was just telling him about the silver bell being stolen."

"Maybe," I said, watching her disappear. There was something still nagging at me. Call it instinct, but it was leading me after her. "Hmm, I fancy a walk, don't you?"

Grandad nodded. "Aye, we will take a wander. See what she gets up to."

We trailed her out of the drive, down the road a bit, and into the village of Brightburgh. I had to walk fast to keep up. My thighs were aching by the time we got there. It was alright for Grandad, he could zoom along at any speed he wanted.

I felt my phone vibrate. It was an antique phone Mum had given me to stay in contact and there was only one number I could dial from it – hers. There was no way to access the internet on it either. I pulled it out to see a text from Mum asking where I was.

2K a walk 2 da village LOLZ, I replied.

'LOLZ' is a daft word Mum uses. It's the kind of thing that would reassure her. Reassure, as in, I'm not on the trail of a potential murderer and there's no serious possibility of me getting bumped off.

She came back a minute later: **OK**. Then she added a whole screen of emojis, each one more ridiculous than the last:

I had absolutely no idea what any of that meant.

At the village green, we watched from the cover of a tree as Lucy pushed through a garden gate, stopping to chat with an older woman who was tending the garden outside.

"That where she lives, do you think?"

There was a kind of everyday familiarity in the way she spoke to the woman that told me she wasn't just a friend or acquaintance. This was confirmed when Lucy pushed through the marigold-coloured door of the cottage and disappeared inside, leaving the woman to continue with her gardening.

"Must be her mum, or something," I said.

I took a pew on a bench under cover of the trees and waited there for a while, but Lucy didn't appear again.

"Come on, let's go up," I said to Grandad.

As I stepped onto the pavement and strolled along the fence, I was sure I saw a flash of a face at the window, but when I looked closer there was nothing. I stopped next to the woman, who was on her knees tending to a bed of sunflowers.

"Hello." I gave her a broad smile.

She looked up at me directly. You can tell a lot from someone's face. For example, from the narrowness of her eyes and her thin lips, I could tell that she was definitely Lucy's mother. The name on the doorplate read:

This was obviously the family home.

She smiled. "Hello there."

"You're Lucy's mum." I smiled back.

"Yes, you're looking for her?" She turned to the door, as if to go and call her.

"No, no!" I waved my hands about. That was exactly what I didn't want. "I'm just one of the guests up at the hotel."

"Oh, yes?" she said, probably a bit puzzled as to the point of this exchange.

A moment of silence.

"*Awk-ward*," Grandad said in a sing-song voice.

"So," I continued. "Here I am, just hanging about. Thought I'd just say hello in passing."

"Well, erm, I'm pleased to meet you," she said.

I held my spot for a beat, still smiling like a maniac. "Do you know the manor at all?"

Her face hardened and her lips narrowed. "More than most."

"Ooh, that was a cold look," said Grandad. "Ask her more."

I gave her my full-on, wide-eyed little-boy look. "I saw Lord Brightburgh. I've never seen a real lord before. Do you know him?"

Her brow creased scornfully, and the edges of her mouth turned down into a scowl. Now she looked even more like her daughter. "Oh, *him*," she replied. "No, he's not very nice."

She turned away, signalling the end of our conversation.

"What you thinking?" Grandad asked.

"I'm thinking... I could murder a roll and sausage," I replied.

A screech of brakes, and Mum suddenly appeared at my shoulder. She was on a bike. And not any normal kind of bike, but a tandem. "There you are, Jay. What are you up to?"

"Just admiring the flowers, Mum." I eyed the bicycle suspiciously. "You don't expect me to get on that thing, do you?"

She slapped the seat behind her and grinned. "I hired this little beauty from the hotel. Now, hop on."

Grandad burst out laughing. "Ha! I think she does!"

She tightened her helmet strap, waiting for me to leap onto the saddle, which I didn't. "Come on! The day is young and we have an abbey to visit."

"A what?" I said.

"They have a beautiful ruined abbey here, just on the other side of the village."

"There's no way I'm getting on that thing." I folded my arms in protest.

Mum beamed. "Fine, you can walk." She pushed down on her pedals and cycled off. "I'll race you!"

Grandad groaned. "Uch! More ruins. More ghosts. I wish I were dead!"

CHAPTER 15

The Deadly Abbey

We popped into the SPAR on the way through the village, but Mum had pedalled off ahead and I only had 59p.

"In my day that was a lot of cash," said Grandad.

"Well, in my day it isn't."

All I could afford was a bag of crisps, which I ripped open and consumed noisily, finishing the lot before we even passed the bin outside the shop. I sighed. "It's no good. I'm still hungry."

We followed the brown tourist signs to the abbey, which sat on the grassy bank of the loch. All that was left of the building was the stone shell of a medieval nave, surrounded by lawns and trees and ancient gravestones.

Mum was sprawled on a grassy bank beside her bike, her ankles crossed, and her face angled up at the sun. "Ahh! The energy in this place, it's magical!"

Grandad, on the other hand, looked like he was about to have a tooth extracted. "This place is HELL!" He gazed around nervously. "It might seem pretty to her, but this place is crawling. There are pure hunners of ghosts here.

Hunners! Here, I will show you." Before I could stop him, he blinked.

Grandad was always prone to exaggeration, but this time I could see with my own eyes that he was telling the truth for once. There were hundreds of them: medieval men-at-arms waving swords, farmers wielding scythes, toothless old hags, one-eyed monks, you name it. They were all glaring at Grandad.

"They do not like the look of me, I tell you. They don't like tourists."

He waved them down with his hands. "Look, I am from Scotland too! I like a good curry, but I also put salt on my porridge. Well, I did when I could still eat."

He blinked again, and they were gone. I sniggered and plonked myself down next to Mum.

"Have you eaten?" she asked.

Despite my hastily eaten bag of crisps, I was so hungry that I practically burst into tears. "NO!"

Humming, she delved into her handbag and brought out something wrapped inside a napkin. What was it? Ooh, a roll and sausage from the hotel? Some bacon? I licked my lips as she unwrapped it.

Grandad burst out laughing. It was falafel. A tiny mound of chickpeas wrapped up in a slightly less tiny parcel of pitta bread. "I picked it up at the wee deli in the village, but you can have it." She smiled at me. "Don't say I'm not good to you."

Yet again, I almost burst into tears. That it had

come to this: being forced to sit in a graveyard and eat something that would barely satisfy a rabbit. But I demolished the thing within about ten seconds anyway. At that point I would have eaten raw seagull if someone had offered it to me.

Mum drew in a deep breath and grinned "Hmm. I think I'll meditate."

"Can I have some pocket money first?" I was thinking about how much it would cost to buy the pork pie I'd spotted in the SPAR earlier. But it was too late, she'd adopted that faraway look that said she'd already vacated the planet and was on her way to a distant galaxy.

Grandad, meanwhile, hunched up his shoulders, as if fearing an attack at any time. "Seriously, I am being threatened by these punters. There is a guy here pointing a giant spear at me. Do you want to see?"

"No!" I wasn't feeling all that comfortable myself. The hairs on the back of my neck were standing on end. But it was nothing to do with ghosts – I was too used to Grandad to be scared of the dead. I felt like I was being watched.

Casting my eye around, I could see one or two tourists wandering the grounds, and a few more descending the metal stairs inside the wall of the nave, which led to a high-level walkway and a viewpoint. But there was no one else in sight.

I got up and wiped my hands on my jeans. "Come on, let's go for a walk."

"Anywhere would be better than this." Grandad's voice quivered.

We skirted the side of the abbey, the stone wall stretching up to my right. "Do you think that receptionist is mixed up in the goings-on at the hotel?" he asked.

"It's possible," I said. "But I'm still not sure how. Nothing gels." In my mind's eye the jigsaw pieces were shifting around in the mist, trying to slot together but never finding the right fit:

* The Yummy Cola letter
* Sharkey's death by soup
* The stolen bell
* The ghostly Grey lady, lady Brightburgh, and her death by gargoyle
* Chase Whitton's death by giant cheese wheel

"It's almost as if..." I stopped.

"What?"

But the thought got away from me, as from right above my head came an ominous crack. I looked up at the wall to glimpse a black-gloved hand, then watched, frozen, as a large section of stone wall hurtled down in my direction.

CHAPTER 16

The Spooky Applause

The pile of rocks plummeted towards me. In fact, they were about to go *through* me. I genuinely thought my number was up, until I felt a body blow against my shoulders, sweeping me sideways.

I tumbled over a stone wall and collapsed, spread-eagled on the grass. The rubble landed with a sickening crunch on the exact spot where I'd been standing.

Grandad was even greener than usual, staring down at his own hands in wide-eyed astonishment. "I... I..."

"You pushed me!" I croaked.

"But... you know... I cannot really move stuff."

I struggled to my feet nursing an aching shoulder, a scuffed hand and a throbbing bump on my forehead. But it could have been a whole lot worse. "You can do it when you want to, and that proves it. You saved my life!"

We were interrupted by the clunking sound of footsteps running down the metal staircase above. "Quick! Whoever pushed that wall over is getting away!"

I ran round the other side of the nave, with Grandad floating beside me, but by the time we got to the entrance

it was too late. All I caught was a flash of black as a figure
disappeared through the main gate and into the trees.

The fall, the shock and the running left me panting
for breath, and I bent double. "OK, so... on top of various
guests and aristocrats being murdered, and the theft of
a priceless antique, now someone is also trying to kill me.
Well, that's just great!"

"On the plus side..." Grandad looked around, smiling,
and pushed up the sleeves of his Mac. "Thanks to my

life-saving push there, I have now got some *serious* respect from these other ghosts."

He blinked again. The ghosts that only five minutes ago had been threatening his very afterlife, were all now standing around Grandad in a respectful circle, their eyes wide with awe. Their weapons – scythes, swords, pitchforks – were cradled in their arms as they nodded and applauded a beaming Grandad.

CHAPTER 17

The Lord's Alibi

I didn't tell Mum about my near-death experience. I probably should have, as I think the bump affected my brain. It must have, because after we left the abbey I quite happily got on the back of Mum's tandem and rode back with her. I'd never have done that in a million years if I'd been in my right mind.

I can't say it was an enjoyable experience. Grandad floated beside us the whole way, pointing at me and laughing. "Oh, if only I had a camera!"

When we arrived back at the hotel I marched straight up to reception. Shand was there, glaring at me like I was something he'd just expelled from his nose.

"When is Lucy on duty again?" I asked.

"Er, she's on split shifts. She'll be back later this afternoon," he replied.

"Hmm." I tentatively felt the bump that was expanding on my forehead.

Grandad, meanwhile, was still staring down at his hands, muttering, "I still do not believe it!"

Having very nearly just joined Grandad in the afterlife,

it was time to get serious about finding out why I was here. Did somebody really want me dead, or had I just got in the way? "Mr Shand, I don't suppose you could tell me who at Yummy Cola you've been dealing with?"

"I'm afraid not," he said. "Everything was arranged in writing. We got a letter, like you did."

"Do you mind me asking how they paid?"

"They paid by bank transfer. That's all I can tell you." He turned away.

"Fine," I said. "In that case, any chance lunch is being served? I kind of missed breakfast... Oh, and dinner last night."

He shook his head. "We've suspended our lunch service for today. Sorry." I could almost hear my stomach crying out in despair. A miniscule falafel wouldn't tide me over for long. "However," he added, "the chef is preparing a special surprise to cheer everyone up. I hope you will enjoy it."

"Any chance that surprise might involve a chicken burger or two?"

"I'm afraid not." He walked into the office, shutting the door behind him.

"A special surprise?" repeated Grandad. "Huh! I bet he is. There is something suspicious about that chef. It is *his* food being poisoned after all. I bet you he is the one doing it. I am going to check him out." Grandad turned towards the kitchen.

"In that case, I might as well do some checking out

myself." I ignored my still-rumbling stomach and turned in the opposite direction.

First, I asked Mum for a loan of her phone.

"What for?" she asked, "and what have you done to your head?"

"Er, nothing, I just bumped it, it's fine. And I want to have a go at Sweet Rush," I said. Sweet Rush was this awful game she was always playing. It seemed to involve barrelling round a massive sweet shop in a trolley, collecting as many sweets as possible, while fairies and goblins attack you from all sides. I wasn't remotely interested in it, but it was a good excuse to get hold of the phone. Hers was a *proper* phone, unlike mine, with internet and everything, and most importantly I could dial out on it.

I ducked outside to the front steps, looking out over the fields towards the ruins haunted by the Grey Lady. The reception was awful, even out here, but I eventually managed to get through to Directory Enquiries.

"Yummy Cola's marketing department, please." I cursed myself, wondering why I hadn't made this call the moment the letter had arrived.

After a short pause, I found myself connected through to Yummy Cola. It was one of those annoying automated response systems, and there were so many options, and options upon options, that I was starting to get confused. I got so bored that I held my nose at one point and put on a funny voice: "If you're eating a cheese sandwich but your uncle *isn't* Bulgarian, please press 3 now..."

At last, I found myself talking to a human being, but I would have been as well talking to a machine. I explained that I was one of the Yummy Cola winners, and I wanted to speak to whoever was in charge of organising the competition, but the woman on the other end of the phone didn't seem to understand. Eventually, after a lot of persuading, she agreed to look into it, then said she'd take my number and call me back.

DI Fallon emerged from the front door, accompanied by a uniformed police officer. He was talking on a mobile, but when he clocked me, he cut short his conversation and put the phone away.

"What are you doing, laddie?" he barked.

Well, excuse me for living! "I'm just standing here getting some fresh air."

"Don't try and fool me, laddie," he said, and leaned closer. "Oh, by the way, you should know that we found some of the stuff that was stolen from reception. It was hidden behind a bus shelter in the village. That's where the hoodies hang out." He snapped his chubby fingers, then flipped them against my elbow. "See, I told you."

"Oh, right, that's good news." I nodded.

"So, in future butt out and let the police do their work."

He stepped towards his car, a blue Jaguar.

"Did you find the bell, too?" I asked after him.

"No, not yet, but it'll be found nearby, I'm sure."

He opened his car door, but I wasn't finished. "So you've arrested them then, the hoodies?"

"What? Oh no, not yet." There was a touch of annoyance in his voice.

I pushed him further. "So did they poison the man who died last night?"

"We're checking that out. The post-mortem is due back tonight."

"And did they push a wheel of cheese on top of Chase Whitton in the cellar in the wee small hours?"

Fallon's face flushed and he stomped back over from his car. His bulky frame loomed over me. "Remember, laddie." He jabbed two of his fingers at his own eyes, then jabbed the same fingers at me. "I'm watching you!"

He opened his car door and smiled – a grey, dour smile lacking in any warmth. "We've got everything under control, so like I said, *butt out.*"

Sure you do, I thought. If hoodies were responsible I'd eat Grandad's ectoplasmic hat. I bet he hadn't even talked to Lord Brightburgh yet, who, despite what Grandad thought, had to be the number one suspect in all this. Fallon zoomed off, leaving me standing on the steps in a cloud of gravel dust.

Lord Brightburgh.

The more I thought about him the more it struck me that he had the one thing I was looking for, the one thing that explained everything: motive. Motive was the thing that drove people to commit crimes. A motive to steal back the silver bell his family had owned for generations? Definitely. A motive to murder the guests? Perhaps. He clearly despised the hotel and hated what Shand had transformed his old family home into. He would love to see it closed down. He had an alibi for the theft of the bell, it seemed, having gone to Edinburgh for the night, but the fact that he'd declared his whereabouts so loudly the previous evening so that everybody in the lobby could hear, made it just a wee bit suspicious.

Evening was drawing in, and distant cattle mooed in the gloaming. My footsteps crunched on gravel as I marched around the side of the manor house.

Five years, I thought to myself, eyeing the ruins – that was how long it had been since Lady Brightburgh's death. I thought about her wandering those ruins, alone and lost. I thought about my dad, too. Grandad said he knew Dad was still alive, that he wasn't 'upstairs', as he put it, nodding towards the heavens. If that was true, then where was he right now? And if that was true, then why hadn't he contacted me? Dead men don't talk, but live ones do. STRICTLY PRIVATE

I paid no attention to the sign marked STRICTLY PRIVATE on the gate. No detective worth their salt pays the slightest bit of attention to warning signs. I walked straight past the line of sunflowers, right up to the yellow wooden door and rang the bell.

The door opened and Lord Brightburgh appeared,

surprised and suspicious. "Yes, can I help you?" he asked, in his clear, cut-glass accent.

Now was the time for a convincing ruse. A good detective always thinks ahead, but with all the wondering about Dad I'd been distracted. I could have kicked myself.

In the gloom behind him I noticed a stag's head hanging on the wall. In my view, only a certain kind of person sees fit to shoot animals and then mount them as a trophy, so I decided to play to it.

"I hear you're an expert in hunting, sir," I said. "I was hoping to ask you a few questions."

He looked taken aback for a second. "Hunting?"

His beagles padded out from behind him and sniffed round my feet.

"Um, yes. It's for a school project. We're all really interested."

Ah yes, the old school project excuse. It works time and time again. They always indulge you, at least for a bit, especially people who are a bit self-important and like the sound of their own voice.

The confounded look hadn't left his face yet, so I acted impressed on seeing the stag's head behind him. "Oh, that's a beauty, sir. Where did you shoot that one?"

Suddenly his face changed. I'd stirred up his ego. "It *is* a beauty, isn't it?" He turned towards it, moving away from the door, and I took the opportunity to step inside.

"Now, let's see, it was one day at my friend's estate in Glen Urquhart..." he droned.

I wasn't actually listening, I was just pretending to. A few nods and smiles in the right places let me snatch some glances at the surroundings while he continued to blather away.

It wasn't a large place, just a few bedrooms, a lounge and a kitchen. Tiny compared to the manor house he'd had to give up. It must've been torture for someone like him, I thought, watching the Shands take over the family pile while he was shunted into the old servant's accommodation at the back. That much was clear from the row of ancient bells hanging from a panel in the higher reaches of the wall, complete with signs reading:

That was how they used to summon the servants. I wondered if they still worked. What if signals could be passed back from the main house to the servant's quarters by an accomplice on the inside? The place was musty, infused with the smell of old varnish, wet dog and cigar smoke. And untidy too. Every surface seemed to be piled with stuff: ornaments, books, bills, plastic bags.

Meanwhile, Lord Brightburgh had just asked me a question, and I had no idea what it was. He was staring at me, expecting an answer.

"Sorry, what's that?" I asked.

"What are you interested in hunting?"

"Oh," I said. "I'm from Glasgow; there's not much to hunt there – just seagulls."

He laughed. "Ha! Too right, pesky blighters. Come along."

He led me down the hall, which was wood-panelled like the main house, and hung with lots of paintings and photographs. Some black and white, others coloured but faded. Old, sombre-looking photos of family going back to Victorian times, and more recent snaps of holidays and weddings. Lots of photos of women: either sisters, mothers, nieces or past wives. I tried to focus on the features, some vaguely familiar, sparking a kind of nagging recognition, but there were too many. There were also a lot of close-ups of flowers, especially sunflowers, and photos of the dogs.

"These are nice photos, sir. And these too." I pointed.

"That was taken by my late wife." He picked up one of the dog photos. "She loved photography. And she loved her dogs."

"And which one is your wife, sir?" I asked, looking round the hall.

He stopped next to the largest of the pictures, a portrait of a beautiful woman with her hair in a neat bob. He gazed at her lovingly. "That's her."

"She's very beautiful, sir." I knew straight away that she was definitely the ghost from up at the ruins. She looked a lot younger in the painting, but it was the same woman alright. The Grey Lady really was Lady Brightburgh.

He led me further up the hall, threading his way through doggie toys and stacks of papers. A room on the right was painted bright yellow, like the front door.

A child's drawings, old colouring books, all curly cornered and crusty, poked out of an open chest of drawers. Some of the drawings were arranged across the top, as if they'd only recently been pulled out.

In the dark and cluttered living room, he sat me down on the only mess-free square of his leather sofa and asked me what I wanted to know about hunting. I thought up a few questions off the top of my head, which weren't very good. He then launched into long rambling answers, which seemed to lead onto long, boring anecdotes. At least it gave me time to think up my next question.

I was hoping to steer him onto the subject of the silver bell being stolen, and his alibi, but I could hardly get a word in. After a while the clock chimed, and he patted his hands down firmly on his knees. "Oh, blast, is that the time? I must get on." He stood up. "I hope I've given you enough for your project."

I stood up too, taking great pains to be super-polite. "Not at all. Thank you for your time." I turned towards the door, then hesitated. "You were away last night, weren't you? You missed all the trouble here. Did you hear about it?"

"Ah, yes. Ah yes, the police, they called at my friend's house in Edinburgh early this morning to deliver the news." If that were true, then Fallon was at least on the ball with something. He'd correctly identified that Lord Brightburgh was the main suspect, and he'd checked out his alibi right away.

"Early?" I repeated.

"Very early. The sun had only just come up." He yawned. If that was true it meant the only way Lord Brightburgh could have been involved in stealing the bell was with an accomplice.

Lord Brightburgh hovered over a large stack of papers

on the bureau. I couldn't see much, but I could make out a few of the larger words, such as 'LEGAL' and 'DEEDS'. I also noticed a few red reminder bills tucked into the pile. Now, for the first time, he looked like an old man. His face had taken on a drawn, confused appearance. He scratched his head. "Er, yes, well, I really must be getting on." Maybe the swaggering was all just a front.

As he shut the yellow front door behind me, I thought deeply about his alibi, and if there was any other way around it. But there wasn't.

CHAPTER 18

The Cyanide Fondue

I passed Granny on the way back to the hotel entrance. She was out near the woodpile, chopping pieces of wood with her own hands. Absolutely *slaughtering* them in fact. There were splinters of wood flying all over the place.

"HI-YAAA!"

I hoped the police weren't watching, because sometimes when a certain glint came into Granny's eyes she looked like a murderous psychopath. From time to time, I wondered if she actually *was* a murderous psychopath.

Inside, the few guests that remained were milling about in the dining room. Mum was there, sitting in a corner with her legs crossed, her hands raised and her eyes closed.

"OMMMMMM!"

This time there was no escape from Mrs Hackenbottom, who nabbed me by the arm as I passed. She had a disconcertingly strong grip for such a frail old lady.

"Have you found anything out, my boy?" She stared at me searchingly.

I didn't want to give anything away, so I settled for something mysterious. "I think there's more to this thing than meets the eye. What about you?"

She leaned towards me and grinned, like a maniacal goblin with false teeth. "Oh, I've done more than that. I've found the murderer."

"Really?" There was no way this smug old nosey parker had managed to uncover the killer already.

"Oh yes, and in the true spirit of an Agatha Christie book, I'm going to reveal who it is once everyone is together. I telephoned the Inspector a moment ago, and he will be here shortly."

At that moment Parek emerged from the kitchen carrying a stack of plates. As the door swung open I felt sure I could hear a muffled ghostly wail from somewhere.

"HELLLLPP!"

Then the door swung shut and the cry stopped abruptly, only for me to hear it again when the waiter returned to the kitchen.

"HELLLLPPP!"

It was Grandad, sounding very much like he was in trouble.

"Grandad?" I said, forgetting I was in company.

"Grandad?" repeated Mrs Hackenbottom, puzzled.

Mum broke out of her trance and patted me on the arm, smiling. "He's in heaven, dearie." She looked at Mrs Hackenbottom, leaned her head to one side and gave a tight-lipped smile. "He's always talking to his grandad."

"How lovely," said Mrs Hackenbottom. "You must have been very close."

"Oh, they were," nodded Mum.

"Oh, you've no idea!" I smiled.

"Oh?" The old lady gave me a curious look.

The waiter emerged from the kitchen again, this time carrying a tray of cutlery and napkins. The sound of wailing returned.

"HELLLLP MEEEEE!"

"Excuse me a sec." I ducked away, gingerly sneaking through the closing kitchen door.

The chef was preparing a couple of large platters. The first one was stacked with cream-topped waffles and pieces of chopped fruit: pineapples, strawberries, pears. In the middle was a steaming pot of chocolate sauce. The second one had chopped vegetables and meat, and little chunks of bread, artfully arranged around a bubbling pot of cheese. This was the famous Swiss fondue, no doubt. It smelt delicious, and I was still so hungry... Focus, Jay!

The chef looked up from his work and eyed me with suspicion. "What are you doing in my kitchen?"

"Er, well..." I sidled along the wall in the direction of the wailing. "I'm writing an article for our school magazine, it's about Swiss cuisine. I was hoping to ask you a few questions?"

Ah, the old 'article for the school magazine' – a slight variation on 'doing a school project', but it worked just as well.

He stared at me for a few seconds, trying to work out if I was joking. The trick was to keep your face serious, open and honest. "You know," I said, nodding at the huge platters, "some say that Swiss fondue is a lost art."

Suddenly, all his suspicion fell away and he sighed with relief, as if at last he'd found someone who understood. "Yes! It *is* a lost art!"

I could hear Grandad's voice nearby. It seemed to be coming from behind a big metal door in the corner of the kitchen.

"HELLLPPP! JAYESHHH!"

"What's in there?" I asked innocently.

"My pantry," replied the chef, at which point Parek returned – or was it Arek? I hadn't yet worked it out which was his real name. The chef lifted one of the platters and shoved it at him, then picked the other one up himself. "Now, I am going to take these beautiful fondues out into the dining room. These will cheer everyone up. No one can be sad when eating Swiss cuisine – it is the finest food in the world. Do not touch anything! I will return in a minute to answer all your questions."

As soon as they backed out with the platters I yanked

the handle on the heavy metal door and dragged it open. My ghostly grandad crawled out, breathless and even greener than usual. He was so relieved he began kissing my feet.

"Thank you! Oh, thank you! Son, I was running out of air in there."

"You don't even need air," I said. "How many times do I have to tell you, you're a ghost!"

"Do not be rude!" He floated into a standing position.

"I don't get it! You saved my life about an hour ago, pushing me out of the way of a ton of falling rock, and now you've gone back to not being able to walk through doors. That's Ghosting for Beginners – Lesson 1."

"I was too tired to even try! You don't understand... Pushing you, that really took it out of me." His greenish face loomed into mine. "Jayesh, you have to listen. It is the chef. You have to stop him!"

"What?"

"*He* did it! He poisoned the food. And he is going to do it again. I saw him take something out of the pantry. That's why I followed him in. I saw the jar myself. It is poison – that one you mentioned last night – cyanide."

"Are you sure?"

"It is poison, I tell you!" he cried.

"But he's just taken the food out..." I turned as the sound of excited chatter rose from the dining room.

"You have got to stop him, boy! Now!"

A good detective should always think before he acts.

On this occasion that's definitely what I should have done, but I didn't. I burst into the dining room, with Grandad close behind. The chef was setting a fondue platter down on the table, the big fancy one with fruit and chocolate and oodles and oodles of cream. There was more oohing and aahing from the guests, and some smiles. One of the German golfers had his camera phone out and was filming it. The chef was right, the fondue was cheering them up, but if what Grandad said was true, that happiness would be very short-lived. There was nothing for it – I had to act, and fast.

"Stop that man!" I cried, and flung myself at the chef's back.

CHAPTER 19

The Splattered Platter

The chef was three times the size of me, at least. I had no hope of bringing him down, but I did manage to knock him off balance. He stumbled forward, clattering against the table.

"AaarGH!"

The fondue platter went flying, vomiting a mixture of fruit, cream and chocolate sauce all over the place: the carpet, the walls, the curtains and people's shoes.

The chef's hat slipped over his eyes, and he staggered about, as if blind. Yanking it back into place, he eyed me with what could only be described as homicidal rage. He grabbed a tiny fondue fork, his knuckles turning white with the strength of his grip.

"I will KILL you!" he snarled, though when he said it in his Swiss accent, it sounded more like "KEEL".

"See!" said Grandad. "He's the keell-er!"

The chef looked down at the splatter of chocolate on his once pristine tunic. "That was my special fondue sauce, made with ci—"

"CYANIDE!" interrupted Grandad.

"Cyanide!" I repeated, for those who were unable to hear the voices of the dead. So, everyone except me.

"He put cyanide in it. He is the poisoner, thank you very much!" cried Grandad.

"Cyanide!?" replied the chef furiously. "CYANIDE? I will KEEL you!"

Parek the waiter knelt down and scooped up a globule of the chocolate sauce from the top of his shoe with his finger.

"DON'T!" yelled Grandad, raising his arms as if he could somehow stop him.

Parek stuck the finger in his mouth and sucked.

"Mmmmm," he said, nodding. "Cinnamony. For once something you have made is actually edible."

"Cinnamony?" I repeated.

One of the German men also scooped up a bit from the curtain hanging next to him and dabbed his tongue with it, before nodding enthusiastically. "*Ja! Cinnamon, ist gut, ja!*"

"Of course it's cinnamon, you fool!" cried the chef.

"Oh, right," mumbled Grandad, looking shifty. He touched the side of his head with his finger, sucked his

teeth, then balanced his hands like a set of scales. "Heh...
cinnamon... cyanide. My eyesight is not what it used to be.
It's an easy mistake to make."

"What?!" I stared around at all the hostile and accusing
faces glaring at me as if, well, as if I'd just spoiled their
only nice surprise on what had been a pretty rotten day.

"Oh, Jay," said Mum. "What have you done?" She
sounded a little bit angry, but not angry enough to stop her
scraping up the last of the cream on the platter with her
finger, then plopping it in her mouth. "Mmmmm!"

I turned to Grandad, shooting daggers at him. "I'm
going to KEEL you!"

I couldn't believe he had been so stupid. I couldn't
believe *I* had been so stupid. I'd just gone and made a
colossal idiot of myself, all because my daft ghost of
a grandad couldn't tell the difference between a common
kitchen spice and a lethal poison. I held my head in
my hands.

"I'm so sorry!"

Shand burst into the dining room. "What's going on?"

Fallon pushed in behind him. Mrs Hackenbottom
seemed to take this as a cue, hobbling into the centre of
the room and dramatically clearing her throat. "I'm glad
you got my phone message, Inspector."

"I drove straight back," barked Fallon, his bushy
eyebrows forming a fierce furry line along his forehead.
"Now what is it that's so important?"

"Well," she said, grinning like the (very old) cat that got

the cream, lapping up all the attention. "I'm afraid this young man here is barking up the wrong tree. For I," she tapped herself on the chest, "Vera Hackenbottom, have discovered who the culprit really is. Yes, *I* have discovered the cold-blooded killer in our midst."

I stared at her, shocked and disbelieving. Had this annoying old windbag actually beaten me to it? Had she gone and solved the crime before me?

Mrs Hackenbottom turned and slowly eyed each member of the assembled crowd. All that could be heard in the tense silence was a few nervous gulps, and one of the German golfers taking a sneaky selfie. A satisfied grin spread across the old woman's face as she stopped, raised her cane and pointed it at a disbelieving Mr Shand. "It was YOU!"

CHAPTER 20

The Wolfsbane Warning

Everyone gasped, not least Shand. "What? *Me*? D-Don't be ridiculous!"

"I wouldn't put it past him!" cried Parek.

"Look in his pockets," suggested Mrs Hackenbottom. "The proof is in there somewhere, I'm willing to bet."

Parek grabbed Shand by the wrist, and the two men struggled. Fallon kept his eyes fixed on Mrs Hackenbottom while the waiter rummaged around in his boss's pockets.

"H-How dare you!" Shand stuttered. "I'm your employer."

"Yes! And a rubbish one at that," Parek replied.

Shand's eyes shot to Fallon, opening out his free hand in a gesture of appeal. "You should arrest this man instead."

Fallon stared back, unmoved, while Shand finally freed himself and turned on his employee. "You and that brother of yours. You're the ones behind this! It's got to be you. Twins are suspicious."

"That's what I said!" chimed Grandad.

I hadn't forgiven him for the cyanide blunder, so gave him a quick death stare before stepping forward. "I'm sorry, but Parek isn't the murderer. In fact, he's not even a twin."

Everyone turned to me, perplexed. "Mr Shand, your waiter, Parek, and your porter, Arek, aren't Parek and Arek at all, they're just Arek. Or is it Parek? I'm not sure." I looked at the waiter questioningly, but was met with a dark glare. "Anyhoo, they're the same person. Haven't you noticed that they're never in the same place at the same time? Haven't you asked yourself why they're always running about with sweat pouring off them? It's hard work doing two jobs at once."

Shand took all this in, then scrutinised the waiter's features. The hotel manager's face whitened and he gasped. "I should have known! One of you was always slinking off. I've been paying salaries to both of you." He turned to Fallon. "Arrest this man! This is fraud!"

The waiter guffawed. "It is Arek, by the way. And both salaries were rubbish! You were not paying either of us enough. Is it any wonder I pretended to be two people?" Now he appealed to Fallon, yelling, "He's the one who should be arrested for breach of human rights!"

"You're fired, both of you!" yelled Shand.

"There's only one of him," I reminded the furious hotel manager.

Mrs Hackenbottom bellowed over us all, a hint of annoyance in her voice, "Now, LOOK! Will you please *be quiet.* I am trying to expose a murderer here!"

Arek went back to rummaging in Shand's jacket

pockets. He found nothing in the outside ones, but succeeded in pulling a small, clear plastic pouch out of the inside breast pocket.

"What on earth!" exclaimed Shand. He looked just as surprised as everyone else.

The contents seemed to be some kind of dried herb, with a white printed label stuck on the front, which the waiter then held up to the light.

"It says: '*Wolfsbane. Warning – poison! Do not ingest, can cause vomiting, diarrhoea, and DEATH.*'"

I'd heard of Wolfsbane. It's a plant, often used as a poison, a potent one – one that was even capable of killing in strong enough doses.

Arek took a cautionary sniff, and recoiled. "Smells awful."

"Here, let me." I leant forward to sniff it. "Woah! That's rancid!"

I turned to Grandad, speaking in a low murmur. "Remember the smell Starkey mentioned before he died?" Grandad nodded. "I bet that's it."

"It's not mine," Shand cried. "I swear it!"

"DI Fallon," said Mrs Hackenbottom, "that is a packet of deadly herbs, which Mr Shand here used to poison the food."

The chef brandished his fondue fork at Shand. "I will KEEL you for poisoning my beautiful food."

Shand backed off. "No, it wasn't me!" He looked from face to face. "It wasn't me, I swear. I mean, why would I—"

The chef came at him fast. Shand whimpered, then turned and fled into the lobby.

Mrs Hackenbottom leaned towards me and flicked her hand. "There you go, you see. That's how it's done. Case solved."

"Smug old bat," grunted Grandad.

Fallon had remained impassive the whole way through. Even now he gave just a narrow smile to the shocked onlookers. "Excuse me." He stepped out of the room.

None of this made any sense, but Mrs Hackenbottom's outburst hadn't altogether surprised me. I caught Grandad's eye and nodded towards the kitchen door. He followed me inside.

"Do you think she is right? Do you think it was Shand?" he asked.

"What, sabotage his own hotel? Nah, I'm still not buying it. If he's really trying to sell then all he'll do is lower the price. Murder is bad for business – he had no motive for killing Starkey or Chase Whitton."

And what about the silver bell? Mrs Hackenbottom hadn't even mentioned it. I could just about buy the idea of Shand faking the antique's theft, although he couldn't sell it on the open market – he admitted himself that it was protected. Maybe if he had an insurance policy on it... But still, I wasn't convinced.

We returned to the dining room, where everyone, including Mum, was congratulating Mrs Hackenbottom for solving the case. Meanwhile, out in reception, the chef was banging his fists like an outraged gorilla on the office door.

"Come out and face me Shand!" he yelled.

Fallon and another police officer were grunting and straining, trying to heave the chef away from the door. Meanwhile a third officer, his teeth gritted, was wrestling with the chef's right hand, which was still armed with the tiny fondue fork.

"PUT. THAT. FORK. DOWN!"

The chef shook the men off and tossed the fork to one side. "Ach! He's not worth it."

He trudged off in the direction of the kitchen, with two of the officers following close behind.

Fallon knocked firmly on the door. "Mr Shand, it's DI Fallon here. Open up."

The office door slowly creaked open and Shand's drawn and red-eyed face poked out. "Is he gone?"

"Yes. I think we need to talk, sir."

"I'm not talking to anyone unless you keep that Swiss lunatic away from me!"

"Yes, OK, OK." Fallon made a patting motion with the palms of his hands. "Stay where you are, I'll check he's secure."

I heard a cough from behind me. It was Granny, standing in her full karate outfit, complete with bandana and sandals, looking like a tiny deranged warrior.

"Ah'll deal with it," she croaked. Then she bowed and set off after the chef. Fallon watched her swagger down the hall with a look of bewilderment. He nodded to the third officer, who reluctantly joined him as he set off after Granny. There was just one officer left now, keeping guard in front of reception.

Grandad took his chance to slip into the office, while I crossed the lobby, smiling at the lone officer and feigning innocence. I tucked myself behind the stairs, waiting and listening.

A minute or so later Grandad returned, shaking his head. "There is something very funny about this. Shand is in there, crying his eyes out. I heard him say, 'I do not understand. It wasn't me.'"

"He's on his own in there, so he doesn't know anyone is watching him," I whispered. "Which means it's not an act – he really didn't do it."

"I noticed something else. There is a contract sitting open on his desk. It is from the Hillingdon Corporation, and it is marked 'Sale of Brightburgh Manor Hotel'. Looks like he is about to sign it as well. He has a pen out, and he is blubbing... something about not having any choice now."

"Hmm, what do you know about Hillingdon Hotels?" I asked.

"In my day," replied Grandad, "it was the world's biggest hotel corporation. They had hotels all over the world. It was owned by some rich billionaire. Oh, what was his name? Connor, I think it was. Connor Hillingdon. He used to be in all the newspapers with his flashy cars and private jets, although if I remember rightly I think he retired and passed the business over to his daughter."

My mind whirred. "The question is – why would a big, seemingly respectable corporation like Hillingdon play such dirty tricks? To get the price down? To force Shand into signing the manor over to them? A big company like that, they don't need the hotel that badly, do they?"

"You are right. I mean, what if they got found out? That would be a big deal, front page news. It does not make good business sense."

"No," I said. "Unless..."

CHAPTER 21

The Karate Granny

"Unless… What?" huffed Grandad. "You keep saying that and then you do not explain! It is very annoying!"

Suddenly, all the jigsaw pieces in my mind floated out of the mist. They hovered tantalisingly close to each other. "You have to stop him signing that contract, Grandad! Now!"

"How am I supposed to do that?" he yelped.

"You're a ghost! Use your ghostly powers. Like you did with me at the abbey."

"Uh! This is exhausting!" Grandad rushed off. Meanwhile, I felt for Mum's smartphone in my back pocket. I still had it, and a good thing too. I plucked it out, then ducked back under cover.

While the phone reception was rubbish, the hotel did have wi-fi, which I swiftly tapped into. Mum never bothers, she just lets her data roaming run out then wonders why she can't get on the internet!

I searched for 'Hillingdon Hotels' and 'Connor Hillingdon'. It seemed Grandad was right – the billionaire had retired a few years ago and given the running of the family business over to his heiress daughter, Vienna Hillingdon. A few more quick searches and it didn't take long for everything to become clear. All at once, the jigsaw pieces slotted perfectly into place.

Stuffing the phone back in my pocket, I heard Grandad making loud blowing noises from the office. He sounded like he was trying to extinguish one of those joke relighting birthday cake candles. I could just imagine his face taking on that slightly reddish shade of green, and his spectral eyes popping out of his head, and his spooky veins bulging out of his temples. I heard a thump as the office door suddenly flew open, and then the sound of fluttering. A massive flurry of paper blew out and scattered around the hall. The police officer on guard looked round, confused.

"AAAARGGHH!"

There was ear-splitting scream from the office. The police officer hurried towards it while Grandad came rushing through him, his face beaming. "Did you see that? Ha!"

"Well done, Grandad!"

Shand's scream brought Fallon storming back into the lobby. It also brought Mrs Hackenbottom, Mum and all the other guests to the door of the dining room. The German men were hooting with laughter at this latest development in their weekend's entertainment. They seemed to be eagerly placing bets with each other as to who the murderer was. Thankfully, I no longer seemed to be in the running. Mrs Shand also appeared, her scowling face poking out of the door marked PRIVATE.

Mr Shand himself came tottering out of the office and groaned weakly. "This place... It's haunted!"

"You bet it is!" hooted Grandad. "By me!" Then he turned to the suit of armour. "Oh, sorry, you too, Sir Bampot."

I eyed something that looked like a legal document among the papers scattered on the floor. Snatching it up, I waved it around and shouted, "Don't sign this, Mr Shand!"

All eyes turned to me.

"You don't have to sell your hotel," I said. "We – I mean, I, not Mrs Hackenbottom – have solved the mystery."

Mrs Hackenbottom folded her arms and wrinkled her face at me. "I already solved the case, young man."

"I'm sorry, Mrs Hackenbottom, but you were wrong. Mr Shand isn't a thief, or a poisoner. And he certainly didn't kill Chase Whitton."

"Then who did, dearie?" asked Mum.

"Well," I rocked back and forth on my feet, my arms clasped behind my back, enjoying the attention, "let's think this through..."

The attention was short-lived though, as at that moment two bodies came hurtling from the direction of the kitchen, locked in combat. The Swiss chef was battling Granny, using a spiky pineapple as a shield and a cucumber as a kind of makeshift sword. Granny karate chopped the cucumber in half, her eyes gleaming.

"STOP!" I cried.

Granny immediately halted her attack. She relaxed and folded her arms inside her sleeves. She wasn't even out of breath. The chef was red-faced and panting. "She... She is a demon!" he gasped. "I think I love her."

"You back off!" cried Grandad. "She is MY girl."

Shand whimpered at the reappearance of the chef and hid behind the desk, while Fallon and two of his officers formed a barrier between the chef and his employer.

I coughed, regaining everyone's attention. "As I was saying, who poisoned the food? Could it have been the chef?" I asked.

"I will KEEL you!" The chef growled at Shand, charging forward like a rugby player.

One of the officers yelled at the other. "Do it!" His colleague yanked out a black and yellow gun and aimed it at the chef.

"Taser! Taser! Taser!" he shouted, and pulled the trigger. Something small and metallic shot out and hit the chef square in the chest. There was a loud crackling noise, and the chef jerked, bolt upright. His face went blank, his eyes rolled up into the back of his head and he started jiggling around on the spot like he was doing a sort of pogo dance. Finally, he toppled over and fell flat on his face.

Granny knelt down, flicked out two fingers, and scraped off some leftover chocolate sauce from the chef's tunic. She smeared it slowly and deliberately across her cheeks like war paint.

Everyone paused for a moment, watching the chef

regain his senses as the policemen cuffed his hands behind his back.

"Orrrrrr," I said, waiting for the eyes to turn back to me, "could it be... Arek, the porter, slash Parek, the waiter?" The party of German golfers parted slightly, to reveal the waiter behind them.

Arek was eyeing Shand too. "I would like to kill *him*."

Mum was standing beside him. She took a step back and gasped.

He held his palms up at her in a show of innocence. "But it was not me, I promise!"

"I told you, you're fired!" screamed Shand, still crouching behind the desk. "Get out!"

Arek was about to pipe up again, but I cut him off. "Look, do you mind? I'm trying to expose a murderer here, and a double murderer no less."

"And you are making a blinking awful job of it too," said Grandad.

"Oh, you shut up as well!" I snapped.

"Eh?" asked Fallon, quizzically. "Who you talking to, laddie?"

"This is your big moment, son," urged Grandad. "Do not let it go."

I coughed, straightened my back and then clutched my hands around two imaginary lapels before pacing around the floor, just like the detectives did in Grandad's ancient TV shows. "I put it to you..." I pointed directly at Mrs Hackenbottom. "Miss *Bleedin'* Marple..."

"My name's Hackenbottom, not Marple!" she cut in.

"Oh, shut up!" Grandad and I cried at the same time.

"I put it to you," I continued for the big reveal, "that **YOU** are the murderer of Brightburgh Manor."

CHAPTER 22

The Viennese Solution

I let my revelation hang in the air for a moment, pacing up and down, as all eyes turned to the little old lady. But Mrs Hackenbottom was unruffled. Her face betrayed nothing as she calmly clasped her wrinkly hands around the top of her cane.

"I put it to you," I added, "that *you* are the one trying to ruin this hotel – so you can buy it."

"What, on my poor old pension?" she scoffed. "What a joke! Look, the boy has obviously banged his head," she pointed to my throbbing bump, "it's obviously addled his brain!"

Grandad leant closer to me. "Are you sure about this, boy?"

Fallon also leant towards me. "Are you sure about this, laddie?"

I ignored them and continued. "Yes, because *you* are not the frail little old lady you make yourself out to be. Oh no, your name is not Vera Hackenbottom, though the initials are the same. I remember seeing them on your case as we arrived. No, *you* are none other than the daughter of famous hotel tycoon, Connor Hillingdon. *You* are the rich heiress, Vienna Hillingdon."

"What?" she replied, unfazed. "A rich young heiress? Look at me, I'm an old woman." She fluttered her eyelids at everyone, bearing a striking resemblance to the mischievous gargoyle Grandad and I had found up at the ruins. Just with a few more wrinkles.

"Not all rich heiresses are young," I countered. "Vienna Hillingdon, judging from a quick search on the internet, is in her fifties. Mind you, she's not as old as you. Or at least, she's not as old as you *look*. I mean, all that hobbling about you do, you poor decrepit old lady. But you weren't so slow when it came to running up the stairs after the porter yesterday, or catching that knife that fell off the table this morning, were you? Don't think I didn't notice."

"Huh!" She turned to Mum. "I saved the boy's knife from falling on the ground, and this is the thanks I get. The youth of today!"

"I didn't even get any breakfast!" I cried. I was officially hangry (anger brought about by extreme hunger). "I have literally had NOTHING to eat since I got to this place, apart from a minging bit of sweaty cheese and a falafel! A *falafel*!"

"You are going off topic, boy," muttered Grandad.

"Topic?" I repeated dreamily. "That's a chocolate bar. I could do with one of them. Or a Kit-Kat, or a Mars bar... anything." My mouth watered.

"Ssshh!" Grandad nodded towards the confused faces. I snapped out of it, turning once again to Mrs Hackenbottom.

"The point is – you let your cover drop," I said.

Mrs Hackenbottom appealed to Fallon, opening out her arms. "Inspector, you're not going to let this boy prattle on, are you? Arrest him."

"For what?" asked Fallon.

"Time wasting, of course."

Fallon said nothing, just turned back to me and nodded.

"He is letting you go on," said Grandad. "Now is your chance, Jayesh. Finish her!"

I strode in front of the old lady and shook my finger at her. "You've been trying to get your hands on this hotel for a while now, haven't you? Visiting here in disguise, you wanted to poison the food, drive away the guests, ruin the hotel's reputation – all so the hotel would have to close down and Mr Shand would be forced to sell. But why, oh why, would a reputable worldwide corporation like yours behave like that? I mean, if you were caught in the act there would be hell to pay, your entire company would be under threat. Why resort to such dirty tactics? It just doesn't make good business sense. Unle-e-e-ess…"

Grandad whipped his hands. "Aw, here he goes again. Unless what?"

"Unless it wasn't business. Unless it was personal. Do you know Lord Brightburgh?"

"Of course not," she replied, but her eyes twitched, betraying something. Was it fear? For the first time, I'd pricked her skin. "He's a lord. I'm just a poor old pensioner."

160

"That's funny," I said, "because when he came swaggering in here last night before he left for Edinburgh, it looked to me like he'd just seen a ghost. And now I'm thinking, maybe he had. A ghost from his past."

A tiny bead of sweat appeared on the old lady's creased forehead.

"I did a bit of digging on the internet. I found a really interesting article on Vienna Hillingdon. It said she'd been jilted at the altar as a young girl, an experience she never forgot. An experience that changed her. It turned her into the ruthless businesswoman she is today. The article also said that both she and Lord Brightburgh went to Cambridge University at around the same time. Funnily enough, there was a picture too."

I held up Mum's smartphone and angled it so that everyone could see. A faded photo showed a young man and woman linking arms and smiling. The man was clearly Lord Brightburgh and the woman was Vienna Hillingdon. Vera Hackenbottom might look wrinkled and old, but the resemblance to the young woman in the photo was unmistakable.

"I put it to you, Ms Hillingdon – since we've established that this is your real name – that it was Lord Brightburgh who stood you up on your wedding day. He was the one who humiliated you, who hurt you. So much so, that years later you're still burning for revenge. You want Brightburgh desperately, because you want, finally, to become the lady of this manor, years and years after he deprived you of it.

You want it so desperately that you'll resort to poisoning the guests to close the Shands down and have them hand the place over to you. What do you say to that?"

She waved her hands around, flustered. But there was no denying it. I had her on the ropes. "This is all... This is nonsense!"

"Well, why don't we bring Lord Brightburgh in here? He can tell us for sure." I looked at Fallon, who turned and waved a finger at one of his officers. The officer departed out the front door, heading for Lord Brightburgh's cottage.

"I don't get it," said Mum. "Is she Mrs Hackenbottom, Ms Hillingdon or Miss Marple?"

I ignored her. I was on a roll now. " *You* were the one hovering over Starkey's table last night when we came into the dining room. I'm guessing you found a discreet way of slipping the wolfsbane into his chicken noodle soup."

"*See!*" came a muffled cry from the chef, who was still lying on his front on the floor with a policeman sitting across his back. "There is NOTHING wrong with my food! NOTHING. Did everyone hear that? Did you?"

Mrs Hackenbottom waved me away nervously. "What rubbish!"

"Oh, is it?" I said. "Cos the article this picture came from was written by an intrepid investigative reporter. I don't suppose you can guess what her name was?"

I turned to Benedict Ravensbury, who was standing, wide-eyed and open-mouthed, watching me. "Why didn't you mention that your friend Chase Whitton was a reporter?"

Ravensbury shrugged and shook his head, confused. "What did that have to do with anything?"

"It was the reason why you were here. Did she tell you that?"

"What? No," he replied. "Chase suggested a weekend up in Scotland doing a spot of hill walking. Now that you mention it, it was a bit unusual for her, given how many times she told me she hated the outdoors, and leaving London for that matter, but I never thought..."

"It was her idea to come here," I explained, "because she was on the trail of a story. She was onto this woman. You, Mr Ravensbury, were her cover."

I gazed round at the faces of the crowd. They were enrapt. I had them hooked. "After Mr Starkey was killed, I found Chase Whitton snooping round in his room. I wondered why, but now it's clear – she was already on the trail of the murderer. And then, in the small hours of last night, some time after the commotion had died down and the police had gone, Chase left her room. She was following Mrs Hackenbottom. She knew you weren't who you appeared to be, she knew about your past with Lord Brightburgh. What she didn't know, as she stepped down the stairs into the cellar, was that she was walking into a trap. Someone was waiting for her." I turned back to Mrs Hackenbottom, whose eyes were now darting about in panic. "*You* were waiting for her. *You* made it look like an accident."

The old lady retreated against the wall as the crowd stepped back in shock. She was crumbling.

"And *you...*" I continued, stepping towards her, "planted that packet of wolfsbane in Mr Shand's pocket."

"And how would I have done that, young man?"

"I spotted you earlier today, crawling behind the reception desk on all fours. Mr Shand's coat was hanging there. That's when you did it."

"Ha!" she cried. "Impossible. I made sure no one was around when I did tha—"

She suddenly halted, her eyes wide.

"She has given herself away!" Grandad cheered. He began to do a celebratory Bollywood-style dance. I was glad no one could see him but me. "That is game, set and match, son."

"A-HA!" I cried.

Fallon stepped towards her. "Ms Hillingdon, I think."

Realising the game was up, something very strange now happened to the old lady. She began to transform in front of the crowd's very eyes. Her back straightened, and she lost her hunch. She began to pull at the sagging skin on her face, peeling it off in ribbons. It had been a very convincing prosthetic mask.

"Yuck! This is making me feel sick." Grandad looked even greener than he usually did. "It is almost as bad as watching that seagull with the penne pasta all over again."

Finally, she reached up, grasped the hair at the top of her head and pulled. Off came the wig and Mrs Hackenbottom's grey curls were tossed to the floor. Vienna Hillingdon's own hair was clasped back against her scalp. She shook it free. It was grey too, though fine and straight, with a healthy sheen.

When she'd finished her transformation, the decrepit old lady was gone. In her place stood a striking woman of about fifty, with high cheekbones and hardly a wrinkle in sight. She flung her cane at Fallon, who raised his arms to block it. "You'll have to catch me first!" she cackled, leaping over the sofa and bolting to the open front door. She was remarkably agile. She even had time to stop and turn, gloating at all the staring faces in the lobby. "I have a helicopter waiting nearby. I'll be in Brazil by tomorrow. You'll never catch me!"

She cackled again, and turned to leave. Only someone was barring the way.

Someone small and fierce and packed full of karate power.

Granny had somehow sneaked past everyone in the commotion. She swung her leg in the air, scything across Hillingdon's chin...

"HI-YAAA!"

...knocking her opponent to the floor. But Hillingdon wasn't finished yet. The heiress staggered to her feet and leapt past Granny.

Grandad took the deepest of breaths and blew, his eyes bulging with the effort.

The front door slammed shut in Hillingdon's face. She crashed into it and fell back, just in time for the pursuing officers to grab her.

"Whoop, whoop!" cried Grandad. "See that karate goddess over there? She's my girl, my girl, my girl." And he continued singing and dancing up the hall. "Look, Jayesh!" He blinked, revealing all the ghosts in the hotel. There was

the man in a 1920s-style smoking jacket that Grandad had told me about, complete with bloodstain. There was the tall hairy bloke in medieval garb carrying a pail of water and wearing a hatchet in his skull. And then there was Sir Bampot himself. They were all looking on and cheering.

"Bravo!" they shouted.

"RRR-RRRR!" cried Sir Bampot through his rotten jaws.

All the ghosts. Except one... the Grey Lady. Her face, sad and desperate, peered in from the lobby window.

CHAPTER 23

The Grey Lady

"So, that is another mystery solved," sighed Grandad.

We were back in my hotel room, staring out the window at the police cars as they drove off into the night, taking Vienna Hillingdon with them.

"Not quite," I said.

"How do you mean?"

Just then, I heard the creak of a floorboard outside the door. A piece of paper had been pushed under it. I picked it up, then flung open the door and peered out, but whoever had left it had already disappeared.

I flipped it open to find a note typed in block capitals:

MEET ME UP AT THE RUINS
IN AN HOUR.

TELL NO ONE.

"Pff!" said Grandad. "Who is it from? What do they want?"

"Oh, I know who it's from," I replied. "You see, I couldn't get everything to fit together. The bell – it just didn't, it wouldn't, it couldn't... unless..."

"Oh, stop it!" cried Grandad.

"Unless there was more than one crime being committed at once, and more than one criminal."

"Seriously? So there's someone else?" He sighed. "I am too dead for all of this. You are not actually going to go, are you?"

"Yes, I am," I nodded. "But with one teensy tiny little tweak to the instructions."

An hour later, I tramped across the grass towards the ruins, shining a flashlight ahead of me. The moon was out, and the only sound to be heard was the distant chop-chop of a helicopter in the night sky.

"Are you sure about this?" asked Grandad. "Could be dangerous. If I let anything happen to you, your granny will kill me."

"Lucky you're already dead."

"That would not stop her!"

I halted in front of the silent ruins, in the same spot we'd been standing earlier that day. I shone the torch towards the trees.

"Look." Grandad pointed back towards the house as a figure approached, also carrying a flashlight. It was Lord Brightburgh, holding up the piece of paper that I'd slipped under his door half an hour earlier.

He stared at me for a second, deeply suspicious. "Well, you wanted to meet. Here I am."

"I know what you did," I announced.

"What the ruddy nora are you talking about, young man?" he replied.

"The silver bell. I know you have it. Where is it?"

He laughed, a nervous, high-pitched laugh tinged with a little bit of panic. "Is this a joke?"

"It must be very hard for you, the possibility of seeing your beloved family estate pass yet again into someone else's hands, like a used car. But to see a ghost from your past return to haunt you, the woman you jilted at the altar all those years ago, Vienna Hillingdon, well, that must have been doubly hard. Too hard in fact. The silver bell was your limit. A priceless family heirloom, and you were determined that it at least would remain yours."

"That's just ridiculous!" he exclaimed. "I have an alibi. I told you, I was in Edinburgh, staying with one of my friends, who, by the way, is a high-court judge. The police came to see me on the morning of the burglary. I was still wide awake and playing bridge when the burglary took place, and my friend confirmed it."

"Hmm." I rubbed my chin. "That's true, very conveniently true, but your accomplice didn't have an alibi."

I heard footsteps behind me, and another figure emerged from the ruins, a female figure in black. She'd added bright yellow streaks to her dark hair.

"Lucy!" Lord Brightburgh looked surprised.

She regarded me with cold, narrow eyes. "My note said 'tell no one'."

I shrugged. "I'm not the only one who can slip anonymous notes under people's doors."

She stalked around me. "You're a nosey boy, aren't you?"

"Ho ho. She is right about that," smirked Grandad.

"No," I replied. "I'm just observant. I notice things. For example..." I turned to Lord Brightburgh. "That moment last night when you came into the reception, when you set eyes on Mrs Hackenbottom, you could see through the disguise right away. You knew it was Vienna Hillingdon. You took Lucy outside on the pretence of needing help loading up your car, even though all you had with you, as I noticed this morning, was a small overnight bag, which you could have easily loaded up yourself. It was at that moment you asked for her help. You made a pact. You asked her to steal the silver bell for you.

"You went off to Edinburgh, as you already planned to do, and spent a pleasant evening with your high-court judge pal. Meanwhile, your accomplice staged a break in at the manor house and nicked your priceless family heirloom, providing you with the perfect alibi."

"Nonsense! I mean, why would she go to those lengths for me?"

"I thought about that. It nagged me for a while, but then it's amazing what you can tell from someone's face if you really look. You have the same eyes, the two of you – icy blue. Oh, and your noses, you've got a kind of aquiline thing going on there. It's quite striking."

"Ah! I see it now." Grandad nodded.

"You could only be related, right? You could only be, what – father and daughter?"

"Lady Brightburgh and I never had any children," Lord Brightburgh protested.

Lucy hissed at him, "Stop it, Father! It's useless. He already knows."

"Yes, a secret daughter, one that nobody else knew about," I said. "When I was in your cottage I passed one of the bedrooms, painted bright yellow, and I saw a child's drawings. They seemed to have been taken out of the drawer and spread around, almost as if you were showing them to someone, persuading them. Did she need a lot of convincing?"

"I didn't need *any*," growled Lucy.

"Lucy, please!" snapped Lord Brightburgh.

"Yup," I continued, turning to the girl, "I recognised your mother from one of the photos in Lord Brightburgh's hall. And I'm guessing you weren't always a goth. Sunflowers, yellow walls, yellow doors, yellow hair." I nodded to the colourful streaks in her dark locks.

Lord Brightburgh's shoulders sank, but he never took his eyes off his daughter. "Yes, yellow was always your favourite colour. And sunflowers were always your favourite flower. She… was my sunshine girl."

They gazed at each other in sadness.

"Wait, the sunshine girl! Did he say 'sunshine girl'?" cried Grandad.

Lucy circled me like a lion about to go in for the kill. "You're a smart guy," she spat.

"Oh, wait," Grandad said suddenly. He was staring at a spot near the wall. "There she is again, the Grey Lady."

"A-ha!" I turned back to the lord. "Lucy might be your daughter, but there's one thing I'm not sure she's told you. Your wife's death. It was no accident."

He stared back, confused, while his daughter stopped in her tracks. "What?"

"She is coming through more clearly now," said Grandad. "Oh, aye, I can see her. She's clearer than she has ever been."

"What is all this?" Brightburgh looked desperately from Lucy to me, and then back again.

"This is where she killed your wife," I explained.

"But… But, my wife died in an accident," he said weakly. "The stones, they fell on her."

I rolled over the broken head of the stone gargoyle with the toe of my shoe. "The wall was pushed from behind. She used a long pole, a bit like the kind you use to shut high windows." I turned to Lucy. "Am I right? Like I heard you say yourself, you're stronger than you look." Then I turned back to Lord Brightburgh. "Once the deed was done, and your wife lay here dying, Lucy simply tossed the pole down the hill into those bushes."

"Yes! That is why the ghost took us down there," said Grandad. "That is where it is. I bet it's still there. If we searched we might still find it."

Lucy was staring at me, her face even paler than usual. "How? How could you possibly know?"

"Toppling walls on people seems to be your *modus operandi...*"

"Ooh, fancy word!" said Grandad. "What does it mean?"

"It means, the way you like to do things," I continued. "Cos you tried the same thing on me down at the abbey today." I touched the bump on my forehead, which was still throbbing dully. "You spotted me spying on you and your father from behind the hedge earlier on. You spotted me following you into town. You spotted me outside your house. And you were obviously troubled enough by my attention that you thought it was worth causing another wee accident. What did you use to prise away the stone?"

She turned towards the ruins and bent down, grabbing something from behind a wall. A metal crowbar. Part of me was a little bit impressed by how prepared she was. Her eyes took on a menacing look.

"Lucy!" Lord Brightburgh exclaimed, shock and horror in his voice.

Lucy stared at him, her blue eyes cold and her mouth twisted in a vicious scowl. "She hated me, your wife. She tried to keep you and me apart. She tried to stop us being together!"

"No! NO!" Lord Brightburgh flung his hands to his head. "I don't believe it! It can't be true!"

Now Lucy turned to me, and her eyes seethed with anger. "You! You're just a boy. Who's going to believe you, anyway, and on what evidence? Either way, I might just have to shut you up all the same."

"Uh-oh," gulped Grandad.

I stepped back towards the crumbling wall.

"Lucy, stop this!" cried Lord Brightburgh.

She stopped and turned to him slightly, appealing with her arms. "You have to understand! I'm doing this so that we can be together."

Lucy turned back to me and advanced, wielding the iron crowbar.

"Grandad! You're up!" I called.

"I cannot stop an iron bar," he said. "No one said a weapon was involved."

"Then stop *her* instead!"

"Ha!" she sneered. "Talking to yourself won't save you."

"LUCY!" yelled Lord Brightburgh, crumbling to his knees.

Grandad puffed out his cheeks and blew, but it was no good. It seemed he'd already used whatever spooky strength he had helping to catch Vienna Hillingdon earlier.

I took another step back, then stumbled over a rock,

falling on my bum. I felt the cold, damp earth pressing up, wondering if pretty soon I'd be underneath it.

Lucy raised the crowbar above her head. "You should have kept your nose out of this."

I had just enough time to utter one final word before she struck. My last word, perhaps, before joining Grandad in the world of the dead.

I shouted it, yelled it, loud and clear, so that it echoed in the darkness of the ruins.

"HOODIES!"

I closed my eyes, clenched my teeth, and awaited my fate ...

The Top-Secret Grandad

An ear-splitting roar and a large gust of wind brought a helicopter swooping over the trees. It hovered above, shining its spotlight down on our heads.

I was expecting to feel the sickening crack of my own skull as the crowbar hurtled down against it, but it never came. I prised my eyes open to find that Lucy wasn't standing over me any more. In fact, she was lying on the ground underneath Grandad, screaming at the top of her lungs.

Grandad leapt to his feet under the glaring overhead light. "YESSS! I totally rock as a ghost!" Then he put his sunglasses on and broke into a kind of 1980s robot dance. It was *not* a good look.

A voice crackled over a loudspeaker. "This is the police. Stay where you are." It was DI Fallon's voice. I squinted up into the light to see his huge silhouette hanging out of the door, speaker in hand. It seemed my code word had worked.

A handful of uniformed officers were running towards us from the manor house. A few more hurtled out of the bushes.

"Phew! That was close, Jayesh," said Grandad.

Lucy struggled to her feet, shaking and panting

hysterically. "Th-th-th-hhis place is haunted. H-h-h-aunted!"

"Ha! Youuu betchya, love!" Grandad grinned.

She pointed her finger at me, accusingly. "Th-th-th-that boy, he's *evil*. He's got g-g-g-h-osts on his side."

"Ooh, she is perceptive, that lassie." Grandad smiled at me.

"That," I said to Lucy, "and I've got this..." I opened my jacket and yanked out the microphone that was taped to my chest. "So now the police know everything." I gazed up at Fallon, shielding my eyes in the spotlight, and spoke into the mic. "Did you get it all?"

Fallon called down through the loudspeaker. "Aye, laddie. She's right though, you *are* a nosy wee boy."

I smiled. I'd phoned DI Fallon the minute I got the note through my door. I told him all about Lady Brightburgh (I left out the ghosty bits, obviously) and we put together a plan that would allow us to catch a thief and a murderer at the same time. In case you hadn't noticed, 'Hoodies!' was my choice of code word for back-up. Oh, how Fallon had loved that. Lucy sank to her knees beside her father, but he pushed her away.

"Murderer!" he snarled.

The uniformed police officers arrived, dragging father and daughter away into the night. Above, I could just make out Fallon raising his hand in salute.

"Well done, laddie. But please, and I mean this in the nicest possible way – I don't want to see you ever again," he said, and the helicopter swooped away.

CHAPTER 25

The Final Question

Next morning, I woke up next to a pair of chicken's feet. At least, I thought they were chicken's feet. But on closer inspection they were actually Granny's, splayed out, shrivelled and bunioned... and poking into my face. At some point during the night she'd given up on her bamboo mat in the corner and squashed into bed alongside me.

Grandad's ghostly head poked through the door. "Ah, you're awake!" He pulled himself through with a particularly loud **SCHLOPP**. "Urgh! I hate that."

He half-danced towards the bed, his hat set at a jaunty angle. "What a night! Me and the boys, we've been having a ball: cigar man, bucket man and Sir Bampot. We have just been chewing the fat, setting the world to rights. You know, this weekend has turned out alright in the end."

My stomach rumbled. It obviously didn't agree given my lack of food over the last 48 hours. I edged out of bed and pulled on my clothes and trainers.

"That was a good night's work, boy," Grandad said as we made our way downstairs to the dining room. Mum and Granny followed behind. "A poisoning, two squashings and a burglary, all solved. I think you have earned yourself a nice big breakfast now. And, hey, with my improving ghost skills I could probably make you one myself."

"It's not quite over," I replied, as I sat down at the table.

He deflated slightly. "What? Don't tell me there's even more?"

I flicked open the Yummy Cola letter. "The invitation. Someone was determined that we come here, so determined they invented a fake competition. We got distracted solving the theft of the bell and the murders, but we still don't know who brought us here in the first place. So, who was it?"

Someone, I thought, who wanted us out of the way, somewhere far from home, far away from any prying eyes. Perhaps someone who wanted to see us, to meet us here. Here in the country, miles away from Glasgow...

Mum had her phone at her ear as she sat down. "Jay, there's a message for you."

I took the phone off her and listened. Only when I

heard the voice did I remember. It was the lady from the marketing department of Yummy Cola. She'd said she was going to get back to me, and here she was.

"I'm so sorry, Mr Patel," crackled the polite voice on the message, "but I've checked with everyone here, and there *is* no Yummy Cola competition. We've never even heard of the hotel. Perhaps you mixed us up with another company?"

My suspicions confirmed, I deleted the message and handed the phone back to Mum. Meanwhile, Grandad was stroking his ghostly green chin. "You know, come to think on it, your father was quite partial to Yummy Cola when he was your age."

Was he indeed...

Arek, now in his waiter's uniform, shimmied out of the kitchen doors with some plates. He was humming and whistling, and for a change there didn't seem to be a single bead of sweat on his brow.

One of the plates was mine, containing a massive serving of fried breakfast: eggs, sausages, bacon, fried bread, beans, the lot. I rubbed my hands and got stuck in. "Shand didn't fire you after all?" I asked around a mouthful of wonderful, delicious food.

"No." Arek smiled. "Mr Shand knows fine well this place would fall apart without me."

He placed the second plate in front of Granny, a dish of carefully prepared *sukiyaki*: a huge mound of sardines with lots of cream crackers artfully poking out. The chef popped his head round the kitchen door, making eyes at Granny. "I hope you enjoy your breakfast, my little Scottish warrior!"

Grandad bristled with anger. For a second I almost thought he was going to lose his ghostly green hue and turn red. He tried to take up a blocking position between Granny and the chef, even though he was a ghost and the only one who could see him was me. "What are you looking at?" Grandad yelled. "She is my girl, not yours, now back off or I'll haunt you!"

He needn't have worried, though. Granny wasn't paying the chef any attention. She turned to the waiter and croaked, "Ah've gone aff that rubbish." Then she pointed at my heaving plate. "Ah'll have whit he's havin'."

"Yes, madam," said Arek, and he whisked the plate away and returned to the kitchen.

Benedict Ravensbury was sitting at his table alone. He stood up, dabbed his mouth with his napkin and stepped towards me, carrying something in the crook of his arm, something green, with the texture of snakeskin.

"I'm off now," he said sadly. "But I thought this should go to you, it's Chase's diary." He placed the book on the table and pushed it in my direction. "You ask a lot of questions. Chase would approve." Then he nodded and left.

I unclipped the cover and flicked it open. Her last entry was dated the night before last, probably written a few hours before her death:

> Searched the victim's room. Found nothing
> of any consequence.
> NOTE — I found a strange boy cowering under
> a table outside. He kept staring at the wall
> when I was speaking to him, it gave me
> the creeps.
> I really HATE children.

"What a nice lady!" I murmured.

After we'd finished eating we wandered out into the lobby to check out. Mr Shand was on his own behind the reception desk, whistling happily. He looked like a new man.

"Och! It's nice to see you with a spring in your step, Mr Shand," said Mum.

"Well, why not?" he replied. "Once the news gets out the TV crews and the reporters are going to be all over this place. It's a perfect time to relaunch our hotel."

"Relaunch?" I asked.

"Yes. From now on it's going to be a murder mystery hotel." Mrs Shand appeared from the office, both ends of a fake knife poking out either side of her head, complete with fake blood. Amazingly, she smiled, and Mr Shand beamed back at her. "It was my wife's idea. I only set up our Facebook page this morning and we've already got loads of bookings."

"Hey, wait a minute," yelled Grandad. He was behind the reception desk, peering over Shand's shoulder at the guest book. "Jayesh! Guess whose name I've just seen?"

Shand laid the book aside and stepped away, giving me a chance to peek over the desk.

There, in amongst a column of Shand's scribbly handwriting, I spotted one name; a name that stood out like a beacon and made the hairs on the back of my neck stand on end.

LYLE OAKEN

The same name from the back of my subway ticket at home, the only piece of evidence I had from the day of my Dad's disappearance.

My mind whirred as we trooped outside and loaded up the van. This was too much of a coincidence. Whoever this Lyle Oaken person was, they were definitely connected to my dad. I knew that the Yummy Cola competition was fake, and that someone had wanted me and my family to come here for a reason – what if Lyle Oaken was that someone? But, what if Lyle Oaken wasn't *just* someone? What if Lyle Oaken was actually my dad? What if he'd brought us here because he wanted to see us, and for us to see him? Maybe he wanted to explain to us why he disappeared, and to let us know that he was alright. Maybe home is being watched, maybe it isn't safe...

So what had gone wrong? Why didn't he let us know he was here? After the murders, and the police swarming everywhere, perhaps Brightburgh Manor wasn't safe either. What would I do in his position? I wouldn't have risked showing myself, not with everything going on. I would just step back into the shadows and wait for another time.

The party of German golfers were packing themselves into a van beside us, on their way to the airport. They were still laughing, joking and singing. Even now, they had no idea the murders had actually been real. I waved at them, wondering if I should ask who had won their bet. They cheered and waved at Granny as they drove off, "Auf Wiedershen, Frau Karate!"

"Now," said Mum with a little sigh, as we all got into the van, "home, home, home." She turned the key in the ignition but Petal failed to start. Mum's face twisted up into a snarl as she turned it over and over again. "Come ON! COME ON! Ya big toaley!"

Finally, the engine spluttered into life, and we made our way down the long drive. Granny flicked through her *Shotokan Karate* magazine one last time, before yawning and tossing it out the window.

Grandad, meanwhile, was peering through the rear window. "Look." He nodded up at the ruins and blinked. The morning mist was rolling through the stones, and the ghostly figure of the Grey Lady was fading. "That's her off now." He pointed his finger to the sky, "She's done what she came back to do. Not me, though." He grinned. "I've still got plenty of life left in me."

Grandad blinked again, and the figure was gone. Or was it? I squinted. Where the Grey Lady had been just a moment before stood another figure. Nothing more than a shape in the mist. A tall, dark figure, with broad shoulders. A man's shoulders. It moved under a tree, just behind the ruins, watching as we drove away.

My heart pounded in my chest and I was about shout at Mum to stop the van, but just as quickly as it appeared, the figure backed away, disappearing into the shadows once again.

"Next time, Dad," I murmured under my breath. Grandad was the only one who heard me say it. "Next time."

"Huh!" he smiled. "Jayesh, with you there is always a next time."

He was right about that. Oh boy, was he right.

TOP-SECRET GRANDAD and me

Jay Patel and his ghost grandad
have another weird and wacky
case to solve in:

DEATH BY TUMBLE DRYER

REPORT

DETAILS:

Since his dad literally did a vanishing act (he's a magician), Jay Patel has turned detective. Now, with the help of his grandad, he's on the case of a dead body that vanished from the library of his Glasgow primary school.

But what do diamonds, blackmail and dodgy launderettes have to do with it?

CLUES:

- A squashed janitor
- A haunted mask
- Some very dirty laundry...

DETECTIVES:

Top-Secret Grandad and me

If you loved Jay and Grandad, try these next!

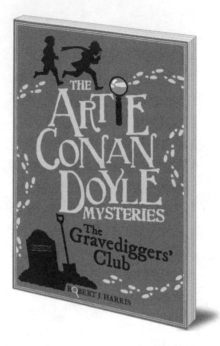

Book 1 in The Artie Conan Doyle Mysteries

A ghostly lady in grey. The paw prints of a gigantic hound. This case can only be solved by the world's greatest detective.

No, not Sherlock Holmes! Meet boy-detective Artie Conan Doyle, the real brains behind Sherlock. With the help of best friend Ham, Artie discovers the secrets of the spooky Gravediggers' Club. Can Artie solve the mystery – or will his first case be his last?

 Also available as an eBook

DiscoverKelpies.co.uk

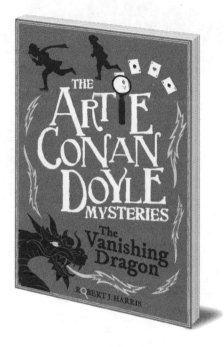

Book 2 in The Artie Conan Doyle Mysteries

Artie and Ham are hired to investigate a series of suspicious accidents that have befallen world-famous magician, the Great Wizard of the North. It seems someone is determined to sabotage his spectacular new illusion.

When the huge mechanical dragon created for the show vanishes, the theft appears to be completely impossible. Artie must reveal the trick and unmask the villain or face the deadly consequences.

 Also available as an eBook

DiscoverKelpies.co.uk

Also by David MacPhail

THORFINN THE NICEST VIKING

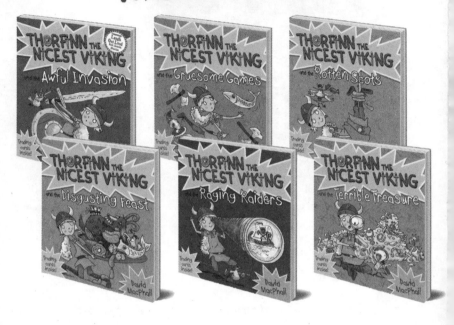

Prepare yourself for the wrath of the Norsemen! That is, if you don't mind and it's not too inconvenient...

Thorfinn The Nicest Viking is a funny and fearsome series for young readers who love *Horrid Henry* and *Diary of a Wimpy Kid*, set in a world where manners mean nothing and politeness is pointless!

 Also available as eBooks

DiscoverKelpies.co.uk